Still a Young Man

Man

Darcy Is In Love

P O Dixon

Still a Young Man: Darcy Is In Love

ISBN-13: 978-1456314057
ISBN-10: 145631405X

I dedicate this story to my dear husband for his patience.

I offer special thanks to Gayle for sharing her exceptional gift!

Contents

Still a Young Man

Chapter 1 — A single man of large fortune

Elizabeth stayed perfectly still while he exercised his prerogative on her person. Her wedding night—the cessation of innocence, happiness, hope, and the life she had enjoyed. Her mother's well-intended advice permeated her thoughts. You must not move ... you must not make a sound ... it will be over before you realise what has happened.

True to her mother's words, the whole business ended almost as quickly as it had begun. She had prepared herself for a most unpleasant experience. Indeed, it had been. Alone in her bed, she cradled her knees to her chest, rocked gently, and looked about the unlit room. Dark, desolate, foreboding.

Her new home. How might anyone endure such an existence?

* * *

Two months later ...

"Why, my dear, you must know, Mrs. Long says that Netherfield is taken by a young man of large fortune from the north of England; that he came down on Monday in a chaise and four to see the place, and was so much delighted with it that he agreed with Mr. Morris immediately; that he is to take possession before Michaelmas, and some of his servants are to be in the house by the end of next week."

"What is his name?"

"Bingley."

"Is he married or single?"

"Oh! Single, my dear, to be sure! A single man of large fortune; four or five thousand a year. What a fine thing for our girls!"

"How so? How can it affect them?"

"My dear Mr. Bennet," replied his wife, *"how can you be so tire-some! You must know that I am thinking of his marrying one of them."*

* * *

Charles Bingley was handsome and gentlemanly with a pleasant mien and unpretentious manners. The folks of Meryton, particularly the ladies of the village of Longbourn, eagerly anticipated making the young man's acquaintance. The upcoming assembly provided the opportunity.

He attended the gathering accompanied by two pretty women—his sisters, Caroline and Louisa. A rather put-upon gentleman, Louisa's husband, Mr. Hurst, rounded out the party. Bingley had heard of the beauty of the Bennet ladies and looked forward to making their acquaintance, as well. All the sisters graced the assembly with their presence, all except Elizabeth. Since her recent marriage, she never attended such public social gatherings. Upon meeting the Bennets, Mr. Bingley suffered no disappointment. Miss Jane Bennet astounded him. She was an angel.

Days progressed into weeks as Bingley pursued an eager courtship with Jane. Proud and conceited, his fine sisters regarded Jane with favour. The rest of the Bennet family, they found detestable. Caroline and Louisa enjoyed far too much satisfaction with their own good fortune to think kindly of others, especially those with connections in trade. Never mind such had been the origins of their brother's wealth, and thus, their wealth and privilege. Being a respectable family from the north sufficed as their proper *bona fides* as fashionable ladies of the *ton*, to their way of thinking. Fondness for Miss Jane Bennet was one thing; it was a different matter when it came to being favourably inclined towards an alliance between the poor girl and their dear brother.

Despite his pretentious sisters' vehement disapproval, Bingley offered Jane his hand, and she accepted. They married two months later. Mrs. Bennet was elated. Two daughters well settled, she considered. Of the two, Jane was by far the most fortunate—her alliance, the most advantageous to the family. Elizabeth's marriage was nothing in comparison to Jane's, Mrs. Bennet often supposed.

Anyone with an inkling of the truth of the matter would have sworn to Mrs. Bennet's assertion.

* * *

The happenings of the months prior to Jane's nuptials to Charles Bingley shed light on Mrs. Bennet's unwitting assertions. The whole town could discern that Elizabeth was enamoured of Daniel Calbry. Unlike Jane, who had known her husband but a few months before accepting his hand, Elizabeth had known Daniel most of her life. The young man had spent a year in London after the completion of his studies. Handsome, amiable, and charming, his return to Hertfordshire was anticipated with eager enthusiasm by the single ladies of Meryton who delighted in his company, Elizabeth more than most. She was pleased to spend time with him and found her head full of him. Thoughts of falling in love with the gentleman often gratified her romantic mind.

To her deep dismay, she had realised the truth about Daniel much too late. She would always remember that day of reckoning, for it had been the turning point in her life.

It was a day best spent out of doors, not confined to one's parlour. She had beseeched her sister Jane to join her on a leisurely stroll, knowing full well the unlikelihood of a favourable outcome. Despite having enjoyed a long walk earlier in the day, Elizabeth set out again that afternoon.

The sounds of what she supposed as someone in peril drew her away from the path towards a thicket of small trees. She espied a young couple sprawled on a tattered woollen blanket spread upon the ground's clearing. Elizabeth's eyes met those of a buxom servant girl with dishevelled hair, her worn brown skirt pooling her waist, astride the man she thought she knew, even esteemed.

Stunned, Elizabeth longed to flee. Her feet failed to heed her mind's screaming, begging her to turn and run away. She fought desperately for her breath. The cold hard look in Daniel's eyes forced her to take a step back. She stumbled and fell, then quickly regained her footing. Fighting to hold back her tears, Elizabeth made her way back to the path in haste.

Bloody hell! He knew he needed to handle this. Tossing the peasant girl aside, Daniel stood and speedily righted himself.

"Miss Bennet!" he shouted as he chased Elizabeth. Her petite stature posed little challenge for his tall person. He soon overcame her.

"Unhand me this instant, you scoundrel," she cried. Her plea was too late.

Merely attempting to restrain Elizabeth from fleeing his presence, and seeking to convince her that she had not seen what she had supposed, he held her in what one might easily construe as a lover's embrace. At least, that is how two passers-by that happened along at the time had described the scene in their later retellings. *Mrs. Long! Mrs. Greene! Two of the nosiest busy bodies in Hertfordshire.*

News spread fast. Word reached the village of Longbourn even before Elizabeth could make her way home. Once she had escaped Mr. Calbry's arms, she raced to Oakham Mount to compose herself and gather her thoughts. *What am I to do? Who will believe in my innocence? My Papa, I must speak with Papa. He will believe me. He will know what is to be done.*

A deafening blanket of silence covered the halls when Elizabeth entered Longbourn House. She sought her father in vain. Her mother and sisters had assembled in the drawing room, each absorbed in her own quiet endeavour. No one, not even her dearest sister Jane, ventured a glance in her direction. Even the dog refused to obey her call. Elizabeth headed upstairs to her room, locked the door, and flung herself on the bed.

Darkness had fallen upon the village by the time of Mr. Bennet's return. He told Mr. Hill to summon Elizabeth to join him in his library post-haste.

Her father's library had always been her favourite room in the house. Leather-bound books organised in no discernible manner competed with potted plants and assorted figurines for the space amongst the shelves and tables. The smell of his pipe bathed the air. It was his sanctuary, but he always welcomed her inside to join him in making light of the world beyond its doors. Mr. Bennet walked about the room, looking grave and anxious in anticipation of her arrival.

"Close the door, Lizzy." She had not expected his cold reception. Elizabeth waited.

"I am saddened and disappointed in you, Lizzy. Nothing will excuse your conduct. Our neighbours caught you in the gentleman's arms. Everyone in Meryton knows he is your favourite. You have brought disgrace upon our entire family."

"I have done no such thing. If you will but allow me to explain what took place, you will realise I did nothing that can be deemed improper." Elizabeth's mind flooded with conflicting emotions—anger and resentment, embarrassment and annoyance —such was her disappointment. How could her father have reached such a conclusion without first hearing an account from her?

"What explanations have you that will negate the damage that has been done? You understand how scandals unfold. Our neighbours happened upon you in your lover's arms. The gossip has spread throughout the town like wildfire. Only one remedy makes sense. I have just returned from meeting with Mr. Calbry. The wedding will take place in one month."

"Never! I will not marry him. I HATE him!" Elizabeth shortened the distance from her father in measured steps. "Papa, I implore you to listen to me. If I tell you what I have learnt of his character, you will not want this for me."

"Hate him, you say? You did a fine job in convincing everyone otherwise—until this very day. I am sorry to hear you say that you hate the young man. However, what does this matter now?"

She wished her former opinions had been more reasonable, her expressions more moderate and circumspect. Her awkward explanations and professions of her contempt for Mr. Calbry might have been spared. Alas, Mr. Bennet had denied her plea for understanding and reasonableness. Elizabeth broke down in tears.

Expressing sympathy for his daughter's predicament, Mr. Bennet approached her and placed his hand upon her shoulder. "Calm yourself, my child. Everything ought not to turn out as bad as you fear. I shall take some comfort in knowing the young man has long been your favourite. Whatever has happened today to cause you now to regard him with displeasure will resolve itself with time. Soon enough, your good opinion of him will return."

He reflected upon his family's plight a moment. He walked over to the window, pulled open the curtains, and stared at the bright moon hovering above his village. "Now leave me to the privacy of my library and go share the news of your impending nuptials with your mama. She will be delighted, even if you are not."

She could not believe it. She would not believe it. Her own father forcing her into a marriage with a man she abhorred and making light of a scheme destined to lay the rest of her life in shambles!

Why has my own father abandoned me?

She was the eldest of five sisters by three years, and though not the most handsome, her charm, her wit, and her intelligence set her beyond the rest. Everyone admired her for her lively spirit and kind disposition and even described her as the brightest jewel of the county. Elizabeth had long enjoyed being her father's favourite. He had considered the remaining women in the house, including his wife, the silliest creatures in all of England, not worthy of any consideration beyond ridicule. He had made all the time in the world for Elizabeth. He had taught her the modern languages and philosophy and encouraged her to pursue her own education in those areas commonly reserved for men, as opposed to the expected delicate pursuits of drawing, needlepoint, and sewing.

Two years earlier, she had spurned a proposal of marriage from her cousin, Mr. Collins. Her mother had been widely in favour of the match because the estate of Longbourn was entailed to the male line, and Mr. Collins was the heir. Her highest aspiration being the marriage of her five daughters, Mrs. Bennet had viewed the prospect of her eldest daughter's marriage as a match destined to secure her family's future. In addition, Mrs. Bennet had believed the advantageous marriage of her eldest would heighten the prospects of the other girls. Elizabeth was at the time nearly four and twenty and well on her way to spinsterhood, in her mother's view. Alas, the man was loathsome and foolish! Elizabeth had sworn she would not have him. Her father had supported her in her decision to reject Mr. Collins.

This made his present stance on the imminent marriage to Mr. Calbry especially difficult to countenance. She rejected the notion her father was protecting her best interest in forcing her to marry. He merely was refusing to take the trouble to rectify her lamentable situation by refuting the town's gossip with the truth.

I shall never forgive him for this betrayal.

Daniel, the second son, had not yet decided which path he would choose in making his own way in life. His eldest brother, Gavin, stood to inherit the estate. Both sons continued to live in their father's home. The father and mother doted on both sons and spoilt them exceedingly. To suppose their son capable of compromising a respectable young lady was inconceivable. Their acquiescence to Mr. Bennet's demand that their youngest son must marry his daughter hardly came without difficulty but rather with deep animosity.

Identical in age to Elizabeth, Daniel never had intended to marry at such a young age. He had meant not to commit to matrimony before he reached his thirties, and even then, he had planned to marry a young woman with fortune and connections. He blamed Elizabeth for his unfortunate circumstances. Under the duress of the forced marriage, he had taken to drink. The strong reek of brandy, heavy on his breath, was Elizabeth's most vivid recollection of her wedding night.

Elizabeth soon came to realise her husband did not wish to lie with her. After their initial *amorous* encounter, he had never returned to her bed. He had confessed when she confronted him that he did not want children. Albeit she did not love him, his revelation distressed her. Trapped in a loveless marriage with no likelihood for children—the prospect was unbearable. His desire not to mate with *her* had not, however, tempered his carnal desires of the flesh, as she had little trouble discerning, judging by the nocturnal sounds emanating on a regular basis from the bedroom adjacent to hers.

* * *

One month after Jane's wedding, came the word of Daniel Calbry's death, a result of a carriage accident whilst on his way home from London. His parents received the dreadful news of their beloved son Daniel's demise, and although devastated by the tragic loss of their youngest son, the family had no compassion for his young widow. They blamed her for their son's restlessness and discontent since the wedding. The forced marriage, together with her paltry dowry of a mere one thousand pounds, contributed to the family's animosity towards her. They wanted her gone away from their home. The only thing they offered Elizabeth, her meagre marriage settlement notwithstanding, was the return of her dowry, certainly not enough for her to live on in comfort.

From a maiden, to a wife, to a widow in the span of six months, Elizabeth worried over her fate. *Where am I to go?* She sat in the Calbry's drawing room two days before Daniel's funeral.

"Jane, what shall I do? I cannot return to my father's home at Longbourn. I have not forgiven him. I never shall. He turned his back on me, outright deserted me, when I needed him most."

Jane placed her hand upon Elizabeth's arm. "Why Lizzy, you must come to live with Charles and me at Netherfield."

"I can barely even imagine such a scheme. You and Charles are just married. Your husband and you should savour this time without an older sister afoot. You need not suffer my burden. Perhaps, I should appeal to my aunt and uncle in town. I thought I might seek work as a governess. They might help me in my quest."

"For you to entertain such a notion is incomprehensible. I will not hear of it. It would break my heart! Do not give the matter another thought." Jane embraced Elizabeth. "Now is the time you need your family most, Lizzy."

Elizabeth was not as grieved by her husband's tragic death as everyone supposed. She neither loved nor revered him. She had been a victim of a loveless marriage, but she would not allow anyone to realise the truth of it. Eager to move on, she was not impressed with her prospects. Should she ever marry again, it would in all probability be to a man either choosing her for her money or wanting her to rear his children. Though she had no money to speak of, nor a desire to raise another woman's offspring, it mattered not. After the horrible experience of her forced marriage, she doubted she would ever marry again.

* * *

A year later ...

Elizabeth jumped out of bed and raced to the window. She drew the curtains back, opened the window, and stuck her head outside. The sun shone brighter than it had in months. The fresh air filled her lungs, warmed her heart, and lifted her spirits.

The first day of the rest of my life!

Moments later, Elizabeth twirled about the room with outstretched arms. She raced to her wardrobe and pulled the doors open.

The contorted grimace marring her beautiful countenance was replaced with a mischievous smile as, one by one, she tossed the detested black bombazine gowns to the floor.

An entire year wasted, adopting the façade of the grief-stricken widow ... no one, not even Jane, doubted the depths of my despair.

As she had done every day for the past year, Elizabeth sought solace in her clandestine plans for her future. *Soon, I shall again have my share of society and amusement—indeed, on my own terms. I am quite decided upon it.*

* * *

Darcy and Georgiana sat across from each other at the breakfast table. As the befuddled expression on his handsome face attested, he struggled to make sense of his correspondence. *He has gone and got himself in over his head ... again!* Darcy was aware of his friend's propensity for falling in love with angels. Now, he had married one. Darcy shook his head in disbelief and placed the letter aside long enough to nibble at his fruit and sip from his cup of coffee. Finding it empty, with a slight lift of his brow, he silently commanded the servant for a refill. Darcy raised the coffee to his mouth, found the rich aroma to his liking, and signalled his approval with a subtle movement of his head. The servant resumed his post by the side table.

"Is that a letter from Mr. Bingley?"

Darcy confirmed his sister's supposition with a nod. "How did you guess?"

"Who else has such power to confound you merely by putting quill pen to parchment? What does he say?"

"Bingley has signed a lease on an estate in such a god-forsaken place as Hertfordshire. He appeals to me to come, for what might be an extended visit, to offer advice and counsel on the management of the estate."

"An estate! How lovely. The first step in the fulfilment of his father's dream—that sounds wonderful. Does he mention the name of his new home?"

"Yes ... Netherfield Park." Darcy's tone held none of the enthusiasm of his younger sibling.

"Netherfield Park," she repeated poetically. Rightly suspecting her brother viewed his friend's act as impulsive, she reached across the table and placed her hand on his. "With such a name, how bad can it be?"

Georgiana smiled brighter than the morning's sun and forced a crack in his stern countenance, a talent she only lately had come to possess. She had not always wielded such an effect on him. They had recently returned to England from a yearlong trip abroad. The time away had proved to be a balm to the two siblings' relationship, which had been strained from the start. Darcy had been resentful at first of Georgiana for taking away his mother. Such was his understanding, formed as a boy in deep mourning.

Only after he had gone off to Eton College did he begin to comprehend that his young sister was not responsible for their mother's death. Lady Anne Darcy had loved children. She had wanted to give her beloved son a sibling. Against prevailing advice to the contrary, she had conceived and given birth to another child after years of failure at the attempt. She never had recovered from the confinement. Mr. George Darcy had suffered the loss of Lady Anne deeply. Brokenhearted, he had not been able to look upon Georgiana with affection. Though surrounded by nurses and maids, she had grown up alone, save the love of a devoted housekeeper, Mrs. Reynolds.

Amidst a household profoundly affected by the loss of a most beloved and cherished matriarch, had lived young George Wickham. He had endeared himself to them all. His easy, unaffected manner had proved a marked contrast to the sober young man recovering from the loss of his dearly loved mother. He easily had ingratiated himself with the elder Mr. Darcy, who came to favour him and placed him on a near equal footing with his own son and heir. Young Darcy had found comradeship with Wickham. Though he was a few years older than Darcy, he had encouraged in the younger boy a sense of adventure. Even young Georgiana had cherished fond memories of Wickham, for he often had devoted hours to her amusement.

When Darcy was one and twenty, his father died, entrusting him with the care of his young sister of fourteen. The sudden loss of his father had thrust him not only into the role of Master of Pemberley at a young age, at a time of his life when the demands of friends and engagements were continually increasing, but also into the position of legal guardian to a younger sister he scarcely knew. Overwhelmed, he had put everything aside save his role as Master of Pemberley. He had relegated the care of his sister to a Mrs. Younge, who lived with them at Pemberley for a period after Georgiana was taken from school, until an establishment was formed for her in town.

Georgiana had been staying in the seaside town of Ramsgate, under the care and supervision of Mrs. Younge, when Wickham travelled there, endeared himself to the innocent young girl, and persuaded her to his scheme. Darcy had arrived in Ramsgate not a moment too soon.

Naïve and excited, Georgiana had told her brother of her impending elopement with George Wickham. Finally, she would have the happiness she had never known as a child. Darcy had been devastated. He had known Wickham was up to no good, but more than that, he was made to acknowledge his younger sister had been unhappy all her life, reared without a mother's love and with a father's neglect and inattention. He had vowed to make it up to her. Only seven years her senior, he knew not what she needed most, a brother or a father. She needed both, but in trying to account for her susceptibility to George Wickham; he supposed she needed a father more ... strong guidance, discipline, fostering, and thoughtful attention.

Darcy had returned to London with his sister, and after securing the services of a well referenced Mrs. Annesley to guide her, they had set off for the continent where they had spent the past year building a basis for a close relationship. He began to look upon her with devotion. She began to regard him as a parent rather than as an older brother.

A month before the timely intervention at Ramsgate, Darcy had ended an entanglement with an older woman in town. Time away from England had served both Darcys well. It had allowed them to become better acquainted with each other, heal wounds left in place from their childhood losses, and distance themselves from those who meant them no good.

"Pray tell, do you intend to accept Mr. Bingley's invitation?"

"He is my closest friend, which obliges me to heed his request. However, what about you, dear sister? Do you wish to travel to Hertfordshire on the heels of our return?"

"Fitzwilliam, do you not recall? Cousin Anne invited me to Rosings Park. I do not wish to disappoint her."

Anne de Bourgh, their cousin, was the daughter of Lady Catherine de Bourgh, his late mother's sister. Darcy's family expected him to marry her. The commonly held assertion was that the two sisters planned the union at his birth. Even his esteemed father had vouched for that fact, but he had encouraged his son to make his own decision in that regard. Darcy's parents had enjoyed a love match. The elder Mr. Darcy had surmised his son might aspire to the same. Darcy was not disinclined to fulfil his late mother's wish. He considered he might marry Anne, but since he was in no hurry, he never allowed that he was open to the marriage to his determined aunt. Lady Catherine equated his silence to tacit consent, and he did nothing to persuade her against the notion.

"Dearest Georgiana, I hesitate to leave you alone for what may be months."

"Brother, you must believe me when I say I will be fine. I love you dearly. Nothing has given me more pleasure than to have spent every day of the past year with you. However, I do not expect this arrangement to go on forever. You have your own life to live. Besides, I have Mrs. Annesley to keep me company."

Darcy conceded the truth of his sister's words. The Ramsgate fiasco haunted him still. In accepting what a grave mistake he had made in forming an establishment for his young sister, apart from his own, he determined that from then on, Georgiana was to reside with him in his London home. Entrusting his sister to the care of Mrs. Annesley, whom he too had grown to revere and trust over the past year, Darcy decided to accept his friend's invitation to visit him in Hertfordshire. He welcomed the opportunity to spend time with his closest friend after such an extended absence, but he dreaded the idea of being under the same roof with his friend's sister Caroline for any long stretch of time. He shuddered in recollection of her overenthusiastic and often inappropriate attentions. As for Bingley's other sister, Louisa, Darcy bore her company reasonably well. Her husband—he mattered not.

Bingley had made it clear to him that his sisters would not be in residence at Netherfield Park during the visit. Darcy released a deep sigh of relief over the information.

At least, that is one bit of good news.

Chapter 2 – She is tolerable

Heavens, these people are strange! What is the purpose of their being here? No doubt, they are awaiting the arrival of a wealthy gentleman to rescue them from their lowly existence. Moreover, what are Caroline and the Hursts doing here? I thought they were in London and would be there for the duration of my visit.

The Bennet women were in lively fashion, fluttering about and bubbling with talk of laces and ribbons, officers and redcoats, and entreaties to Jane and Bingley to hold a ball at Netherfield.

Mr. Darcy had captured the attention of the room by his fine, tall person, handsome features, and noble mien. Questions arose from every direction.

"How do you find Hertfordshire? Do you dance, Mr. Darcy? What say you about a ball? Do you not think it is an excellent idea?"

Sick of the obsequious air of the room and annoyed because so much effort was made to garner his opinion on this thing and that thing by the silly young Bennet ladies, Darcy escaped from the room on the guise of handling some business with his man but with an unsettling conclusion: his friend had attached himself to the most uncouth lot of people he had ever had the misfortune to encounter. He indeed had seen a collection of people in whom existed little beauty and no fashion, for none but one of those whom he had met had held the smallest interest for him.

Mrs. Bingley, she is pretty, but she smiles too much.

Upon his precipitous departure from the room, Mrs. Bennet's opinion of the young man had been established. At first glance, she had thought him a suitable match for either of her unmarried daughters, save Elizabeth, but in the wake of his exit, his character had been decided. He was the proudest, most disagreeable man in the world.

"The shocking rudeness of Mr. Darcy, he is above his company and above being pleased. I quite detest the man!" The startled speeches amongst the Bennet women rang out vehemently. The most violent against him was Mrs. Bennet, whose dislike of his general behaviour was sharpened into particular resentment by his having slighted her daughters.

* * *

The stately Netherfield library, widely regarded as the finest in the county, made for a perfect refuge from the raucous goings-on in Bingley's drawing room. Endless rows of shelves lining the rich mahogany walls were stacked with pristine journals, most of which had never been cracked, a silent testimony to the lack of interest displayed by the estate's current residents. Though nothing compared to the library at Pemberley, its atmosphere calmed Darcy's strained sensibilities. Darcy appreciated the reprieve.

His long legs crossed, Darcy settled in a comfortable chair across from his friend. Bingley sat on the edge of his seat. A thousand questions flooded his thoughts on how Bingley's life had suffered such a turn.

"For Heaven's sake, how did you find yourself here?"

"Netherfield Park is a fine estate, do you not agree?"

"I imagine it is as fine as any other. You miss my meaning entirely. I do not speak of the estate. I speak of your alliance with this *Bennet* family." Darcy spat the appellation disdainfully. "In your letter you mentioned nothing of their connections, their fortune. What do they have to recommend themselves, pray tell? What were you thinking?"

"The Bennets are one of the finest families in Hertfordshire."

"What about the father? What is his manner and deportment? He cannot be beyond reproach if his wife is any indication."

"Mind you, Darcy, it is my family of whom you speak."

"As I will endeavour to consider," said Darcy, barely contrite and urging Bingley to answer his question.

"Mr. Bennet is a fine gentleman. He commands respect wherever he goes. I might add he is somewhat reclusive. He rarely ventures beyond the village of Longbourn nowadays. He does not visit Netherfield, but perhaps he will be persuaded to attend the ball, then you might meet him and judge for yourself."

"Longbourn? Am I to assume *Longbourn* is the name of his estate? Does he have a son who will inherit the property?"

"No, Mr. Bennet has no sons. The estate is entailed to the male line of the family. Jane's cousin, a Mr. Collins, will inherit."

"My God! Do you mean to say you are one heartbeat away from supporting the lot of them?"

"Indeed, I am, if you choose to see it as such."

"What were you thinking in taking on such responsibility?"

"You spoke with my Jane. Tell me that you do not think she is an angel."

"I grant you that she is pretty. Her family, on the other hand, is quite another thing altogether." Darcy thereafter went on to explain that he had found them ... unrefined, vociferous, ill-mannered, and unfashionable.

"But what about Jane's sister, Elizabeth? I dare say she is pretty, as well."

"I think 'tolerable' best describes her," Darcy quipped. *Elizabeth.*

"Tolerable? Surely, you jest. I would not be as fastidious as you are for a kingdom!"

Indeed. Darcy had found it hard not to admire her. "I stand corrected, my friend. I seldom have beheld anyone more stunning than she." Darcy altered his manner and tone dramatically in recollection of his initial impression of Elizabeth—her pleasing figure, her long dark hair, her eyes. He uncrossed his legs and leaned forward. "What can you tell me about her?"

"Nothing, besides the fact she lives at Netherfield with us. Beyond that, I shall not discuss my sister with you or anyone. If you want to know anything more, you shall have to ask her."

Elizabeth chose that moment to make her presence in the library known to the gentlemen. They had been unaware she was seated comfortably in an oversized chair facing the fireplace, engrossed in a book upon their arrival and thereby privy to their entire conversation.

Whatever does he mean in questioning my brother on my situation? Saying, on the one hand, I am tolerable, and, on the other hand, I am stunning. The insolence of that man! I shall have to keep a sharp eye on him. Elizabeth approached the gentleman, obliging him to stand. *He has a satirical eye. If I do not begin by being impertinent, I shall soon grow afraid of him.*

"Mr. Darcy," she stated. She curtsied and quitted the room.

Darcy's mask of indifference belied his embarrassment. She had heard everything! Either she was offended because he first referred to her as tolerable, or she was flattered because he had described her as stunning. Neither of the two bode well, in his opinion.

Chapter 3 – Rendered uncommonly intelligent

Stunning indeed! Having had a chance to observe Elizabeth some-what riled, Darcy found her face was rendered uncommonly intelligent by the beautiful expression of her dark, wide eyes and long lashes.

Darcy determined to uncover everything he could find about Elizabeth. To his dismay, other than Caroline and her sister Louisa, he had no one to aid in his quest. Darcy abhorred reverting to the one tactic he felt certain would encourage them on the subject.

"I wonder Miss Bingley, how do you find Mrs. Bingley's sister, Miss Elizabeth Bennet? She is an amiable young lady."

"Amiable? Hardly—her manners are quite lacking indeed, an abominable mixture of pride and impertinence."

Louisa concurred. "Beyond being an excellent walker, as you shall see for yourself soon enough, she has nothing to recommend her."

Caroline chimed in once more. "Eliza, a *young lady*? Come now, Mr. Darcy. Why surely you must be aware she is the eldest of the Bennet daughters. She is at least seven and twenty. She can hardly be called a *young* lady. Do you not know she is a widow, barely weeks out of mourning?"

"A widow? No. I had no idea. Surely, you are mistaken regarding her age. She does not look a day over one and twenty. She must have been quite young when she married."

Caroline seized her chance to portray Elizabeth in the worst light possible in discussing the particulars of her story with Darcy, at least according to her understanding.

"Mind you, Mr. Darcy, as a rule, I would not repeat a word of this to anyone, but since you are a particular friend of the family, and she is a part of my brother's family, after all—" Caroline leaned in closer and lowered her voice a tad. "She was caught in a scandalous act with her lover. Her father forced the gentleman to marry her.

"I say *forced,* but one might as well have called it a love match. She had made no secret of her tender regard for him. The alliance, no doubt, devastated his family, for she had no fortune, you see, while their eldest son's bride had a dowry of fifteen thousand pounds," Caroline embellished.

Louisa longed for her share of such disparagement. "No Caroline, I do believe you are mistaken. Why I heard the amount was twenty thousand pounds."

"Oh, no matter. The material point is our dear Eliza had nothing. The family threw her out of their home before her dead husband's burial."

Darcy was ill prepared for the sisters' account. "Her situation is most unfortunate. You say it was, in truth, a love match."

"Oh, I am convinced of it, for poor Eliza mourned the loss of Mr. Calbry to the detriment of everything else. Our dear Jane gave up her first Season in town, as Charles's bride, to remain here with her. I sincerely doubt poor Eliza should ever recover from her disappointed hopes."

"Married ... no, widowed," he voiced softly upon escaping Caroline and Louisa. *Unfathomable! When Bingley made the introductions, he simply referred to her as his sister Elizabeth.* Darcy felt great remorse for his earlier comments to Bingley. *She overheard everything, every disparaging word. How unfeeling she must think me!*

Darcy was eager to make amends for his earlier slight of Elizabeth. He decided to show her more kindness and consideration than was his wont with strangers. With her arrival in the drawing room in time for dinner, he approached her.

"Mrs. Calbry." He bowed.

"Mr. Darcy." She curtsied.

"May I have the honour of escorting you to dinner?" He extended his arm to her.

"You may, sir." She accepted his proffered arm and proceeded with him to the dining room. Darcy assisted her in sitting, thereby affording him a chance to lean in closer than propriety dictated.

Lavender. He chose the chair next to hers.

Darcy spent the larger part of dinner focusing his attentions upon Elizabeth, much to the disappointment of Bingley's sister. She could not discern what Elizabeth's appeal might be. She employed her wit and charms in every way in her power to divert his attention towards herself, but he could be impressed with Elizabeth only. Elizabeth, on the other hand, was far from impressed with him. The overheard conversation had taken root in her fertile mind. No amount of flowery talk was apt to eradicate it.

Darcy was captivated. Discoveries equally unsettling succeeded his earlier recognition of the beautiful expression of her dark eyes. Despite Caroline's assertions of her manners not being those of the fashionable world, her teasing wit and easy playfulness fascinated him.

Darcy sat closest to Elizabeth at the card table, to her increasing uneasiness. Darcy partnered with Bingley and Elizabeth partnered with Jane. Bingley's sister was perplexed, for in all her acquaintance with Mr. Darcy, when did he ever join in such pursuits without being cajoled into doing so?

With Mr. Hurst napping on a sofa near the fireplace, across the room at a comfortable distance from the others, sat Bingley's sisters. Feigning disinterest in the lively card game, they spoke in hushed whispers.

"Mr. Darcy makes no secret of his preference for our dear Eliza, and quite brazenly, if you ask me. He has not strayed from her side for more than a few moments. He hangs on her every word, and he attends her most fervently. I can never recall him as being so attentive to any other woman before. I suppose it must be the allure of an older and *experienced* woman that enthrals him." Louisa lifted her brows to emphasize the suggestive nature of her remarks.

"Why, whatever do you mean? I detect no preference for her from Mr. Darcy—no more than he shows me, I grant you."

"Caroline, you may be able to fool yourself with such an assertion, but you cannot fool me."

"She does not hold him in any esteem."

"Not esteem Mr. Darcy? Impossible! Mrs. Calbry, you must realise, is clever—clever indeed. She spurns his attentions to her advantage, for even a man such as Mr. Darcy is most impressed with that
which he cannot have."

"I am sure I do not know your meaning, dear sister."

"Yes, I am sure you do not, dear Caroline." Louisa decided to
leave off the conversation. There were some things to which her maidenly younger sister should not be privy, and while she had heard rumours of Darcy's former amorous attachment in town, she did not
intend to discuss said rumours with Caroline.

* * *

Darcy observed Elizabeth most intently over the next few days, hoping
for a chance to know her better, but always thwarted in that attempt by
the constant presence of others. Bingley's sister would not allow that he
should enjoy more than a few words with her, even during meals.
Forced to study her from afar rather than engage in private conversation, he sensed something was not right. The beautiful Mrs. Calbry harboured some secret. Indeed, something that seemed to him to be most
distressing to her. Whatever it might be, Darcy was determined to discover the truth.

One day, Darcy came upon Elizabeth alone in the library, standing
by the fireplace, a brown shawl draped around her shoulders. She bore
a look of discontent, incompatible with the countenance he had come
to expect after regarding her behaviour amongst others.

He approached her and tenderly placed his hand under her chin to
lift her face. "My dear Mrs. Calbry, are you all right?"

The gentle touch of his hand sent a curious shiver of excitement
through her body. She brushed his hand aside and moved a slight distance apart. She endeavoured to smile. "Yes, I am fine. Nothing is
amiss, Mr. Darcy."

Darcy clasped his hands behind his back to resist the urge to reach
out to her again. "Mrs. Calbry, you must pardon my saying so, but I
think you are saddened. Might I help?" Elizabeth looked away.

"Though you and I scarcely know each other, I can be a sympath-
etic listener. I offer my services to you. It might help."

"I assure you, sir, it is nothing. I am taking a reprieve from the gathering."

Darcy's gentle concern was reflected in his piercing blue eyes and his calming voice. "Is it your grief over your late husband? Perhaps you are not yet comfortable in society."

"No—it is not that. I have honoured the required period of mourning. It is time I venture back into society."

"Not necessarily. People grieve in their own way, and not according to a timetable or the dictates of society or convention. Though, on some levels, you may long for a return to normalcy, you cannot force it. If you are not yet ready, it is not unheard of. Take your time."

"I thank you for your concern, but as you said, we barely know each other. Furthermore, I have no wish to discuss such personal matters with you. Excuse me, Mr. Darcy." Elizabeth walked away. The late autumn afternoon's warm, setting sun was much preferable to her current company. She headed outside for a breath of air.

Elizabeth soon came upon what had become her favourite spot in the park. She always headed there for quiet reflection. She took a seat on the wooden bench, intending to stay for a while.

In my haste to flee Mr. Darcy's company, I neglected to bring my book. Overbearing, rude, pompous man! Elizabeth kicked a pebble across the path. *Shall 'presumptuous' be added to his list of faults?*

She gathered herself and headed along the path. *I was correct when I surmised Mr. Darcy has a satirical eye ... an eye that is always fixed upon me. I shall exercise extra vigilance in his company. I will not suffer anyone's pity. I shall triumph over this.*

Chapter 4 – All the best part of beauty

No one looked forward to the Phillipses' dinner party more than Elizabeth—her first outing since her husband's death. She was a combination of excitement and nervousness. She missed the days of her light-hearted maidenhood.

The occasion afforded Darcy his first opportunity to socialise with the inhabitants of Meryton. Had he tried, he might have enjoyed a modicum of ease amongst their society. He did not. When he spoke, it was largely to members of his own party, which included Elizabeth. She noticed he seldom veered far away from her. She soon suspected he was listening to her conversations.

After using her witty repartee to mercilessly tease and charm a new acquaintance, Colonel Forster, she parted his company with proof of her suspicions regarding Mr. Darcy's behaviour.

What does Mr. Darcy mean by listening to my conversations? First, my aunt and uncle, and now Colonel Forster. This stops now! She approached Darcy with impertinence. Her witty inquiry on his thoughts on her request for a ball, sounded rather like flirtation, filling its happy recipient with pleasure. He thereby responded in kind. Elizabeth was hardly flirting with the haughty gentleman. She would not allow him to think otherwise.

"I must say, Mr. Darcy, I detect a strong interest on your part in my conversations. Many young ladies, worthy of the consideration of a young gentleman such as you, are in attendance. Perhaps you might focus more upon them and less upon me."

"Perhaps, but I am not interested in speaking with any other lady tonight. You are the only woman who commands my attention, at present," said he with a measure of flirtation of his own as he leaned towards her.

"Mr. Darcy, please, try to remember yourself. Your attentions might flatter a young maiden in want. As I am not, you might better spend your time otherwise engaged." She turned abruptly and, with a swish of her silk skirts, walked to the other side of the room, leaving a shocked Darcy standing there. He never recalled having been so summarily dismissed by a woman in his life!

Redcoats sprinkled every corner of the room. Kitty and Lydia gaily adorned the arms of the prettiest amongst them.

The young girls had made the handsome gentleman's acquaintance earlier that week, while on their daily walk to Meryton. So impressed were they that they had spoken of little else other than his handsome face, excellent figure, and pleasing address. They had beseeched their aunt and uncle to have a dinner party to which he must be invited.

When the two ladies approached their eldest sister, their unrepressed giggles betrayed any pretence of their being decorous.

"Dear Lizzy, have you met Mr. Wickham?"

Indeed, she had not. Then again, Elizabeth had not required a formal introduction to the handsome officer, for his reputation had preceded him by the earlier accounts of her younger sisters.

I appreciate my sisters' enthusiasm! She offered her hand. "I am delighted to meet you, sir."

He graciously raised her hand to his lips and imparted a lingering kiss across her knuckles. "Charmed, I am sure." Elizabeth returned his enchanting smile. To her younger sisters' dismay, she accepted his proffered arm and soon was the happy woman by whom he seated himself.

Darcy had been in another room when the officers arrived and returned to see Elizabeth enthusiastically engaged in conversation with Wickham. The hairs on the back of the officer's neck stood on end when he espied the tall gentleman.

"What is that self-righteous cad doing in the wilds of Hertfordshire?" Wickham muttered under his breath. Elizabeth's eyes followed the course of his to behold Darcy entering the room. She, in observing the countenances of both as they looked at each other, was all astonishment at the effect of the meeting. Both changed colour—one white, the other red. Bestowing a look of utter revulsion at the situation before him, Darcy returned to the room he had just exited. The animosity between the two men was impossible to dismiss, and Elizabeth sought to know more. Spared the unhappy prospect of presenting herself a meddler, she was relieved when Wickham broached the subject himself.

"I was not aware Mr. Darcy was here in Hertfordshire. Are you much acquainted with the gentleman?"

"Indeed. He is a guest at my brother's home, Netherfield Park. I take it that you know the gentleman, as well." Elizabeth was eager to hear from the man who had robbed Mr. Darcy of his composure. "He is a man of rather large property in Derbyshire, I understand."

"Yes," replied Wickham. "Pemberley ... Indeed, it is a noble estate. I once considered it my own home, for I have been connected with Darcy's family from my infancy."

Elizabeth's countenance confirmed her astonishment. "You may well be surprised, Mrs. Calbry, at such an assertion, after witnessing the cold manner of our greeting."

Wickham began to tell Elizabeth the story of his long and unfortunate history with Darcy, increasing her fascination with each passing minute. The more he spoke, the more closely she listened. From what she knew personally of Mr. Darcy, none of what was said should have come as a surprise.

Does my brother know what manner of man he calls his best friend? By his account, but for Mr. Darcy's selfishness, his jealousy, and his callousness, Wickham might not be an officer. The church ought to have been his profession. The late Mr. Darcy, his godfather, had bequeathed him a valuable living; but when the living fell, Darcy had given it to someone else.

"Good heavens! You mean to say he disregarded his father's will? Did not you seek legal redress?" Such was her dismay in hearing Wickham's account of the informal terms of the bequest and of Darcy's giving the living to another, she decreed, "How shocking! He deserves public disgrace."

Wickham assured Elizabeth he would never defy or expose the younger Darcy as long as he esteemed the memory of the elder.

Surely, there is much of honour in such a man, Elizabeth considered. Wickham's tale of woe extended to Darcy's family, his younger sister, his aristocratic aunt, Lady Catherine de Bourgh, and the lady's daughter. The sister, he pronounced proud and haughty ... the image of her brother.

The one topic she found most astounding centred upon Darcy's esteemed aunt, Lady Catherine. Wickham asked Elizabeth in a low voice whether she had heard of the venerable aristocrat. She acknowledged that her ladyship had bestowed a living upon her cousin Mr. Collins.

"Lady Catherine de Bourgh and Lady Anne Darcy were sisters. She is Mr. Darcy's aunt. Her daughter, Miss Anne de Bourgh, will one day have a large fortune at her disposal. Darcy and she will unite their two estates in marriage."

Elizabeth's ensuing smile was one more of pity than amusement. *Poor Caroline, does she not know her attentions towards the proud gentleman are for naught? On the other hand, what of Mr. Darcy's attentions towards me? What should I make of it?*

Elizabeth allowed that Wickham had given a rational account, and upon their parting, she went about until dinner with her head full of him, and thoughts of nothing but of what he had told her.

Later in the evening, an opportune moment arose for Darcy to speak with Elizabeth. He seized a spot next to her when her sister moved away.

"You were blessed with the honour of spending the evening with Mr. Wickham. How fortunate you are." His voice teemed with condescension and sarcasm.

"Indeed, such a delightful diversion, considering some of the other gentlemen here tonight," she replied saucily with a tilt of her head, referring to her present company.

Darcy hardly took offence to her impertinence. "He is favoured with such happy manners; he is sure to give pleasure to anyone so predisposed. However, I would caution you to be careful where that gentleman is concerned."

"Allow me to remind you, sir, you are not in a position to caution me." She balled her fist and released a frustrated sigh as she stood and walked away.

Caroline had kept her eye on Darcy the entire evening. She sidled beside him in the wake of Elizabeth's hasty leave-taking.

"I do not suppose you will enlighten me as to what just happened, Mr. Darcy?"

"I should imagine not."

Caroline would not be dissuaded. "Mr. Wickham is a favourite of our dear Eliza. I wonder if we might soon be wishing her joy. What say you, Mr. Darcy?"

One glance at Darcy's furrowed brow might have told Caroline everything she needed to know of his opinion on the matter. Darcy spoke not another word in response. The last thing he wanted was to encourage her long flowing vitriol.

I would not bet on that.

* * *

The party at Netherfield passed many evenings in the drawing room engaged in various pastimes as playing cards, reading, and exhibiting on the pianoforte. Caroline's relentless attentions to Darcy had become a sport in itself in Elizabeth's view. Often, Elizabeth was distracted by Caroline's antics, to the detriment of her own doings.

"Is Miss Darcy much grown since last year?" Caroline asked.

"Indeed, she is now about Mrs. Calbry's height, or rather taller."

Must he always reflect his comments upon me? Elizabeth doubled her efforts to attend to the book she was reading.

Soon the conversation veered from the accomplished Miss Georgiana Darcy to the definition of accomplished women in general.

Caroline's litany was lengthy as she pranced about the room, refusing to stray from Darcy's general proximity. "A woman must have a thorough knowledge of music, singing, drawing, dancing, and the modern languages, to deserve half the word *accomplished*." She took a seat beside the object of her esteem and smoothed her dress. "In addition, she must have a certain something in her air and manner of walking, the tone of her voice, her address, and expressions, to deserve the word fully."

Darcy often had observed that Elizabeth spent much of her time reading, case in point as evident that exact moment. He seized the opportunity to draw her into the conversation.

"Indeed, and to all this, she must yet add something more substantial, in the improvement of her mind by extensive reading."

It worked!

"With such a list of accomplishments as that," replied Elizabeth as she hastily closed her book, "I wonder at your knowing ANY accomplished women, Mr. Darcy."

"On what basis do you doubt my assertion, Mrs. Calbry?"

"I never met a woman with such capacity, taste, application, and elegance, as you describe, united."

Darcy responded haughtily to Elizabeth, "Might I assume then that you compare your experience in such matters to my own? I, for one, am far more exposed and certainly more experienced by virtue of my role and responsibility as Master of Pemberley, my knowledge of the world gained through extensive travels, and even my gender, I dare say—whereas the only claim to such knowledge you can reasonably boast of is what you have read in books or garnered by the rather limited society of Hertfordshire."

"On the contrary, I have spent enough time in London to dispute your claim. I have met many acquaintances."

"Under the watchful eye of your aunt and uncle, and through the sheltered eyes of a young maiden, no doubt. Or do I presume too much?"

Elizabeth cast Darcy a knowing eye. "Heaven forbid, who would accuse *you* of being presumptuous?"

Elizabeth stood and mimicked Caroline's manner of walking about the room and fawning over the gentleman.

"To deserve the word, one would have to take it upon oneself to interfere in the lives of others, thinking he or she knows something of the other person's situation. One must even go as far as to decide the fate of others, according to one's own dictates, to lord over others as judge and executioner.

"Indeed, I, for one, would never accuse you of being presumptuous, Mr. Darcy. You are safe from me."

Later that evening in the privacy of his apartment, Darcy considered he was making progress in his quest to know Elizabeth; however, it was not the kind of progress he desired. Then again, what hope did he have with Caroline's constant presence? If not Caroline, then Mrs. Hurst. He had to admit to the excitement of their verbal skirmishes. Darcy thought she was the most bewitching woman he had ever met.

Safe from her indeed!

Elizabeth, on the other hand, was becoming more put off than pleased by Darcy's obvious attention to her person, and suffering, first-hand, its effect upon Miss Bingley. *Poor Caroline! Is she totally unaware of Mr. Darcy's attachment to his cousin?* Elizabeth began to suspect Darcy's motives. *Is he paying so much attention to me in an attempt to discourage Caroline's affections? If so, surely he must realise it is not producing the desired outcome. Caroline's determination increases each day.*

Louisa also covets Mr. Darcy, though far more discretely. Elizabeth smiled. *With such a husband as Mr. Hurst, one can hardly blame her, even if the object of her desire is the arrogant Mr. Darcy.*

Soon Elizabeth's thoughts wandered to Kent, specifically Rosings Park. *What sort of young lady is Miss de Bourgh?* She recalled her sycophantic cousin, Mr. Collins, as having described his esteemed patroness's daughter as a most charming young lady, perfectly amiable, though of a sickly constitution. Elizabeth supposed it was just as Mr. Wickham had said.

Mr. Darcy is marrying his cousin solely to combine the two estates. He does not care a fig for his cousin. He is no different from any other man.

Chapter 5 – Your own wilful ignorance

F ew occasions engendered more excitement and promise than the prospect of a ball. The night of the Netherfield ball was everything it ought to be. The full moon loomed over the country lanes, rendering safe passage for all who ventured out in pursuit of the evening's gaiety. The crisp air was accommodating, and the stars glowed as brightly as the glint in Elizabeth's eyes. Her first such soiree in over a year and a half held much promise. What a delightful evening it would be! She thought with pleasure of dancing the night away, especially if a certain Mr. Wickham was in attendance.

Room by room, Elizabeth made her way through the sea of white gowns and black tails, searching in vain for Mr. Wickham amongst the mass of red coats assembled. She never considered he might not attend. Elizabeth had high expectations for the evening. She had dressed with more than usual care and prepared in the highest spirits for the prospect of delightful conversation and ardent mutual admiration throughout the evening. Though she had spoken with Jane in her quest to make sure the gentleman would be invited, it dawned on her that perhaps Mr. Darcy had persuaded her brother, his steadfast friend, otherwise.

In due course, her sister Jane approached her. "My dearest Elizabeth, Mr. Wickham is not here. He was called away to town."

A likely story. "Jane, I suspect the presence of a certain gentlemen makes it impossible for him to attend."

"Whatever do you mean?" Elizabeth had told Jane a little of the sordid history between Mr. Wickham and Mr. Darcy. "Surely, you do not suspect Mr. Darcy of having anything to do with Mr. Wickham's absence."

Elizabeth had no time to respond. Darcy approached Elizabeth to claim the promised set. He had observed her less than subtle search for her absent friend. He was displeased in the extreme. In the course of their dance, they remained for some time without speaking a word. She began to imagine their silence was to last the entire set. Resolving to say something to the taciturn man, she remarked on the general pleasantness of private balls over public ones. He replied shortly and was again silent. After a pause of some minutes, she addressed him a second time.

"I suppose you deserve credit for the absence of Mr. Wickham this evening."

Darcy guarded his expression, if not the tone of his voice. "You take an eager interest in that gentleman's concerns."

"Who that is aware of his misfortunes can help taking up his cause?"

"Of course—the gentleman held you enthralled on the evening of your relatives' dinner party. I suppose he plied your lovely head with lies about me."

"Pray tell, if I am not to rely upon the word of your childhood friend, how else am I to sketch your character? Am I to depend upon Miss Bingley's adorations alone?"

"You might start by asking me, rather than resorting to gossip."

"In other words, I should not use the same tactics you employed to learn of my situation."

"The difference is in who was consulted and for what purpose. I sought information from your brother, someone who knows and respects you, whereas you, madam, sought information on me from someone who made no secret of his hatred towards me."

"You, Mr. Darcy, are a hypocrite. You find nothing wrong in prying into my affairs, yet you object when I behave likewise."

"No, Mrs. Calbry, you are the hypocrite, for not only did you engage in a derogatory conversation regarding my affairs, you relished in it." His patience waned. His temper flared. "How can you consider that scoundrel's words against me, uttered upon your initial meeting with him, when you have known me for weeks?"

"On the contrary, Mr. Darcy, I know little if anything about you."

Darcy endeavoured to atone for his earlier show of displeasure. "Then, I shall endeavour to correct the situation, starting now, if you would allow me to escort you to supper."

"I shall allow no such thing. What with us residing at Netherfield under the same roof, what would people say?"

"I beg your pardon, madam, for the apparent breach in decorum in suggesting we dine together tonight, as we have done every night for the past weeks," he said sarcastically.

"You are pardoned, sir. No doubt my sacrifice will be appreciated by the young maidens in attendance tonight."

"If you insist, Mrs. Calbry," Darcy submitted, annoyed by her continuing insinuations that he was unworthy of her regard, by virtue of either his age or possibly her marital status. She said no more, and they completed the dance and parted in silence.

Denied the privilege of escorting Elizabeth to supper, he sat opposite her. Had either of them chosen, they might have spoken at length. They did not. The lack of discourse between the two did nothing to lessen the discomfort that they and everyone else who had the opportunity to overhear Mrs. Bennet's conversation with her neighbour, Lady Lucas, suffered. To the masked vexation of those accustomed to her silliness, she still boasted of little other than her daughter's excellent match and of Bingley's being such a charming young man ... so rich, living but three miles away. She complained of the inconvenience she suffered lately in not being free to visit her dear Jane daily, as had been her wont prior to the arrival of a certain proud and pompous young gentleman.

Elizabeth was upset by her mother's lack of etiquette and restraint. Its surest effect was the solidifying of Mr. Darcy's low opinion of her relatives. While she had never consciously done anything to garner his good opinion, she did not like his having added cause to look down on any of her family. He was Bingley's closest friend, after all. She was ashamed her mother had marked him an intruder upon her own felicity.

Elizabeth's chagrin was worsened by the outlandish behaviour of her two younger sisters. Kitty and Lydia flaunted, effusively, their unladylike attentions to the officers, while Mary exhibited on the pianoforte to the amusement of all. Darcy had not been aware Mr. Bennet was in attendance that evening until he witnessed the reclusive man approach his daughter and interrupt her exhibition with a badly managed admonishment that she should let the other young ladies exhibit. Darcy was curious of his insensitivity to his middle daughter and wondered why he showed no inclination whatsoever to check the inappropriate behaviour of the two youngest.

Overall, Bingley was oblivious. Jane was serene. Gleeful, Caroline and Louisa supposed this must cast a different light in Darcy's mind regarding his admiration of a certain young widow. Elizabeth was mortified. However, she need not have suffered on Mr. Darcy's account. She only needed to look his way to realise that he bore her no ill will nor held her accountable in any fashion for the indecorous behaviour of her family.

* * *

The day after the ball, Darcy was out for a solitary ride. While passing through Meryton on his return to Netherfield, he spotted Elizabeth standing in front of a shop speaking with George Wickham.

Darcy dismounted from his horse. Without preamble, he approached Elizabeth and her companion. Startled, Elizabeth supposed he had taken leave of his senses in interrupting a private conversation. Darcy stood next to Elizabeth, facing his nemesis with his face drawn in a dark scowl.

"Mr. Wickham, I am certain you can have nothing more to say to Mrs. Calbry. Leave us now, before you find yourself in the LAST situation you would wish to encounter."

Elizabeth forced her mouth closed. His audacity had no bounds. Altogether unprovoked, in her view, Mr. Darcy had issued a blatant threat. Everything Mr. Wickham had said about the gentleman was true. Under the circumstances, she uttered the most tactful response she could muster.

"Mr. Darcy, Mr. Wickham and I are in the middle of our conversation. Will *you* excuse us?"

Wickham had already contemplated his escape. "Mrs. Calbry, perhaps it is as the gentleman suggests. We had better part each other's company, for now. We are sure to meet again. Good day, madam." He bowed before scampering off.

She clenched her tiny fists by her sides. Elizabeth's temper flared. "How dare you embarrass me as you did, Mr. Darcy? Who do you suppose you are?"

"Mrs. Calbry, I think it is better if you are not seen in the company of that gentleman."

"What care have I about what you think?"

"You SHOULD have a care! I will not conduct this conversation with you in the street, but you need to understand certain things about the gentleman who has captured your fancy. If upon hearing what I have to say, you decide he is worthy of your friendship, I will no longer interfere.

"I will see you back to Netherfield Park. We shall finish this conversation there. May I assume you at least came here by carriage, as would have been appropriate, or did you walk to Meryton alone?"

"For your information, Mr. Darcy, I am here with Jane."

"Where is she? I shall escort you to her at once."

Upon her return to Netherfield, Elizabeth sought Darcy straightaway. She found him in the library, absorbed in the book before him.

"Pardon me, Mr. Darcy." Elizabeth waited, arms crossed. His brow furrowed. His eyes met hers, begging her purposes. She did not cower. "I demand you explain yourself this minute."

"I have every intention of explaining myself, madam." Darcy closed his book, stood, and walked to the library door to close it. He offered towards a comfortable chair while he elected to stand. "Will you have a seat? This conversation is long overdue." He began to walk about the room, his hands firmly clasped behind his ramrod straight back.

"When I first observed you and Mr. Wickham speaking intimately, I allowed you the benefit of the doubt. I trusted your power of discernment to recognise he is not someone whom one takes seriously and certainly not a person whom one trusts.

"Your exhibition in the streets of Meryton this afternoon proved otherwise."

"How you do go on with your vague warnings and innuendos about poor Mr. Wickham. You demonstrated to me today that everything he accuses you of is true!" Elizabeth was furious. She took leave of her chair and closed the distance between them. "You are arrogant and conceited with a selfish disdain of the feelings of others.

You are the last man in the world I would trust to recommend anyone's character!"

Her cutting words took him aback. With cool civility, he asked, "Why is your opinion biased against me, based upon that man's word, when you only met him? You have known and resided under the same roof with me for weeks." The two now stood face to face.

"I base my opinion of you on more than just his word alone. From the first moment of my acquaintance with you, when you maligned my family to my brother and questioned him on the wisdom of his marrying my sister, my dislike of you was established. I can scarcely believe a word you say."

"Mrs. Calbry, I have been an acquaintance of Bingley's far longer than you have, and I know him far better than you ever will. I am his closest friend! I have the right to question his motives and to speak to him as I did. You were wrong to remain in the room without making your presence known to us, enabling you to overhear a conversation obviously intended between trusted friends.

"Bingley invited me to his home to offer advice and counsel. What I did was in service to a friend."

"What about Mr. Wickham? Did you not also consider him a friend once? How can you explain your callous behaviour towards him?"

"I do not know what lies he has told you. I do not wish to know. Nevertheless, I will share my family's history with the man with you. Should you persist in your eager attentions towards him, I will not interfere."

"I am not sure I want to hear anything you have to say about him. He is kind and amiable and gives pleasure wherever he goes, whereas you only give offence!"

"Mrs. Calbry, I apologise for any offence to you and your family. However, you must admit, the situation I witnessed, when introduced to your mother and your younger sisters, was appalling. Would you have expected me to rejoice in such inferior circumstances for my friend? I have since seen how happy Bingley is. I would wish for nothing more.

"Trust me when I say you do yourself and your family a disservice in openly displaying your preference for Mr. Wickham. He is not a man you should trust and a continued association with him will harm your reputation."

"What evidence exists in support of your claims against him?"

Darcy ran his fingers through his dark, curly hair out of sheer frustration. Did he dare trust her with the truth? He had no choice. Once he had made a start, it was only right to tell her all.

"If you will allow me, I will tell you the whole of his connection with my family. I only ask you to keep what I am about to confide in strict confidence." Though Elizabeth said nothing, Darcy took her silence as tacit consent to his terms. He beckoned her to return to her seat.

"My father loved Mr. Wickham—" he began. He told how his father had made a bequest of a living to Wickham upon his death. Darcy explained why he had viewed Wickham in a much different light than his late father. The vicious propensities—the lack of principle, which he was careful to guard from the knowledge of his patron —could not escape the observation of a young man of nearly the same age as himself and who had opportunities of observing him in unguarded moments.

Darcy told her how Wickham had refused to take orders and demanded the value of the living instead. He had been given three thousand pounds, which he gambled away. When he had been refused more money upon his subsequent return to Pemberley, Wickham's resentment towards Darcy had turned into something viler, even evil. Wickham had sought revenge then, as now.

Darcy had no way of telling if anything he said to Elizabeth made a difference. She sat in complete silence. He continued his account.

"Having said this much, I suffer no doubt of your secrecy. My sister, over seven years my junior, was left to the guardianship of my mother's nephew Colonel Fitzwilliam and myself. The woman who presided over her London establishment accompanied her to Ramsgate. Mr. Wickham went to Ramsgate, as well, with the intent of persuading my sister that she was in love and consenting to an elopement. She was not yet fifteen, which must be her excuse; and after stating her imprudence, I am happy to add I owed the knowledge of it to her. I joined them unexpectedly a day or two before the intended elopement. Georgiana, unable to support the idea of grieving and offending her closest family member, admitted the whole scheme to me." Darcy wrung his hands, his anguish displayed on his face.

"Mr. Wickham's chief object was unquestionably my sister's fortune of thirty thousand pounds but I cannot help supposing the hope of avenging himself on me was also a strong inducement. His revenge would have been complete indeed.

"This, madam, is a faithful narrative of my history with the man. I hope you believe me and acquit me henceforth of cruelty towards Mr. Wickham. I cannot stand by and allow him to take advantage of you, knowing so well as I do the mischief of which he is capable.

"Good day, Mrs. Calbry." Darcy quit the room without waiting to ascertain how his words had affected her. He did not wish to know. That Elizabeth held Wickham in such high esteem yet cared nothing for him was too much to bear. He only prayed she would be wise enough to heed his warning.

Elizabeth was taken aback by Darcy's revelations. What once had been deemed certain was now muddled. Did she dare to believe a word he said? How might she do otherwise? Surely, Mr. Darcy would not disparage his own sister. She unconsciously took up his manner of pacing the floor. Her mind raced.

Mr. Wickham, the handsomest, most agreeable man I have met in the longest time ... a scoundrel.

All at once, she ceased her frantic pacing back and forth, gripped with the sudden realisation that her late husband Daniel had always been described exactly as she had described Mr. Wickham—charming, amiable, and pleasing. Why had she not recognised it sooner? Did her obvious dislike of Mr. Darcy blind her to the faults of Mr. Wickham? Did her obliviousness signify something deeper?

It occurred to her that she had perceived Wickham as a victim, forced into a life of misfortune pursuant to the whims of the privileged few. However, if she were to give credit to Mr. Darcy's assertions, then she must allow that Wickham was no victim. His fate had been of his own choosing. Much like her own, she considered briefly before banishing the notion from her mind. Though her situation was certainly not of her own choosing, she was no victim either. She would not be pitied by anyone.

Back to the matter at hand, she recalled how mistaken she had been regarding Daniel Calbry's character. Perhaps Mr. Darcy's words held merit. *Mr. Wickham is not worthy of my trust after all, but what of Mr. Darcy himself?* She still vividly recalled his initial words ... tolerable, stunning.

He scrutinises my every move. Is he trustworthy? Is he simply a young man who finds himself inexplicably drawn to an older, worldlier woman?

Shall I consider him harmless?

Chapter 6 – In the way of other rich men

Months had passed since the day of Darcy's precipitous leave-taking of Netherfield Park. His early dawn departure had been on the heels of his argument with Elizabeth. Had he joined his hosts at dinner during his last night as a guest in their home, he would have found Elizabeth conspicuously absent. Neither had been eager to spend time in the other's company. Time and distance was what Darcy had felt he needed. Bingley's impertinent sister-in-law had robbed him of his composure long enough.

The dawn of spring ushered in such hope for a particular inhabitant of Longbourn Village. What plans Mrs. Bennet had concocted! A Season in London, she reckoned, would suit her quite nicely.

Jane had been far too unconvincing when telling her mother it would not do. Mr. Bingley was determined he would not celebrate that time with anyone but Jane, and Elizabeth, of course. The inclusion of the younger girls would hardly be beneficial. The younger girls must simply await their turns.

When the Bingleys, the Hursts, Caroline, and Elizabeth travelled to town, a decidedly put out mother-in-law did not bother to participate in their send-off. Mrs. Bennet had bragged incessantly to her neighbours of one of the particular advantages of Jane's marriage—it would put the rest of her girls in the path of other rich men. She was vexed over this missed opportunity, especially because the first possible prospect had failed miserably on account of the proud Mr. Darcy. Surely, he would be the exception, she often considered, for what man could fail to fall in love with one of her daughters, especially her dearest Lydia. The girls had suffered no inconvenience by the disappointing outcome, what with so many redcoats about. Lydia and Kitty had time for little other than regular jaunts to Meryton, and Mary could not be bothered to look up from her books.

The Season in town was a cause for gladness for Elizabeth, and not simply owing to the abundance of prospects for gaiety. It also meant she would no longer be in the company of the Bingleys' excellent sisters every day. Caroline had chosen to live with the Hursts on Grosvenor Street since Bingley's marriage to Jane. Neither Caroline nor Louisa was particularly fond of the company their brother kept. He delighted in entertaining Jane's relatives from Cheapside. Likewise, he enjoyed being entertained by them. With no chance of seeing Mr. Darcy until he returned to town from Kent, they preferred other more socially advantageous venues for entertainment.

* * *

Ah, Rosings Park at Easter! The occasion of being abroad had prevented his visiting the year past. Darcy descended from the carriage ahead of his sister and cousin.

I have missed this place. Darcy was always happy to visit with his family in Kent. But for the fact his memories of the month spent in Hertfordshire the past autumn had haunted him and caused him to question his long held tenets on familial obligations, he would have suffered no reservations this visit. The more he thought upon it, the more he began to question the wisdom of a marriage to his cousin, one of convenience and duty, when a marriage of love was starting to become more appealing with each day.

Thank Heavens I never did or said anything to suggest to Anne that I had even considered a marriage to her before. The time away from Hertfordshire had done little to erase the memory of Bingley's sister-in-law. Instead, it had convinced him that he simply adored her.

Allowing what he perceived as a deep sadness in her, he had to concede that she possessed a deep sense of passion, as well as compassion.

Yes, compassion—what else might explain her susceptibility to George Wickham's lies. Something beyond her obvious dislike of me must exist to account for her fervent defence of the scoundrel. He could only imagine the falsehoods Wickham had spread. He prayed Elizabeth would take his words of caution to heart and allow for their veracity.

Darcy also felt she possessed a generous spirit and had suffered much pursuant to the tragic loss of her husband. He dreaded the notion she might suffer heartbreak once more. He was pleased when he learned from Bingley that Elizabeth was in London with Jane and him, far away from George Wickham's society.

As much as she does not care for me, I am unable to persuade myself not to care for her.

Unlike prior visits, two others completed the Rosings Park party this time around. Lady Catherine made sure to include her clergyman, Mr. William Collins, and his wife, Mrs. Charlotte Collins née Lucas, several times for tea.

One afternoon, Lady Catherine raised her head in a regal stance and peered about the room before settling her attention on her parson.

"Mr. Collins, I have told you that my nephew had occasion to visit Hertfordshire."

"Indeed, your ladyship." The bumptious man adjusted his dinner jacket and turned towards Darcy. "Perchance you made the acquaintance of my fair cousins, the Bennets of Longbourn, Mr. Darcy?"

Darcy searched the registers of his memory until his conversation with Bingley encroached. *Mr. Collins. The entail.* "Yes, of course. I had the good fortune of staying at Netherfield Park."

Collins puffed out his chest. "And Longbourn ... did you by chance visit there, as well?"

The audacity of this man! Can he not wait until Mr. Bennet dies before demonstrating this vulture's pride of ownership?

Darcy was prevented from uttering a response when Lady Catherine demanded her share of the conversation.

"I am informed your friend, Charles Bingley, married one of the Bennet daughters. I had rather supposed he would have set his aspirations a bit higher. Though she may indeed be a gentleman's daughter, I understand her father has no fortune to speak of, and many of her close relations are connected in trade."

And your point being? Darcy wondered if he had spoken aloud as his aunt pontificated on how Bingley would have better connected himself to a reputable society family, should he ever one day hope to minimise his own dubious claims as a gentleman. She conceded that perhaps his choice to let an estate was indeed a wise decision, and she praised Darcy for taking the young man under his wing.

To Darcy's dismay she continued, "Darcy you are so much like me in that regard, always looking out for those less fortunate than you, and doing everything you might in helping them order their lives and raise their own lot in life."

Darcy looked at his aunt strangely. *Heaven forbid! Order other folks' lives! Me?*

Lady Catherine looked around to include her nephew, Colonel Fitzwilliam, in her praises. "Though Darcy's choice of a bride is settled, I am sure *you* would never align yourself with a young woman whose relatives have ties in trade."

Soon enough Lady Catherine directed her attention back to her parson, to the relief of Darcy and the colonel. Darcy observed the sycophantic behaviour of the odious Mr. Collins towards his aunt.

Are all of Elizabeth's relatives ridiculous? He coloured. He had not meant to disparage his friend's wife.

Elizabeth and Mrs. Bingley, I must exclude. That said, two diamonds in a heap of rubble do not a treasure make.

A week into his stay, Darcy's enthusiasm in being amongst his relatives waned. True, he was glad to see Georgiana and Anne getting along so well. The young ladies, both a tad shy, enjoyed each other's company immensely. With the increasingly pleasant weather, Anne and Georgiana often rode about the park in Anne's phaeton. They took many opportunities to call upon Mrs. Collins at the parsonage, as well. He found Mrs. Collins pleasant enough. Mr. Collins, he found quite the opposite. Besides, the London Season was already underway. Though it had, theretofore, held little appeal, this year was different. Elizabeth was there.

As Darcy sat at dinner with his family one evening, his distraction evidenced as he pushed his food around on his plate, he wondered if those weeks of his visit would ever end. He smiled inwardly as he listened to his rather opinionated aunt prattle on about the business of the families in the parish. He considered how some people, the Bingley sisters specifically, had described Elizabeth as haughty and opinionated.

If my memory serves me correctly, she IS rather headstrong, judgemental, impertinent, and even a little impetuous. Darcy smiled. *I think it is wonderfully refreshing. She is unlike any other woman of my acquaintance.*

Lady Catherine was as pleased as ever to see Darcy that year. She was sure each visit brought him closer to fulfilling his duty to his family and offering for Anne. However, having seen no more progress during this trip than when he had left close to two years ago, she began to grow apprehensive.

Just prior to his departure, she took him aside and offered words of counsel.

"Darcy, I have done my best to remain quiet as year after year, you continue to put off the inevitable. I have allowed for your education. I waited patiently as you acclimated to your role as Master of Pemberley after the death of your father, and I even countenanced your impulsive trip abroad with Georgiana. You might have considered taking Anne along, by the way.

"Though you are still a young man and at leisure to take your time regarding these matters, my Anne is of an age where she might have been married long ago. I implore you to do your duty."

Chapter 7 – Of ten times his consequence

D arcy descended his well-appointed landau and looked around. Crested carriages lined the brightly lighted street.

And so it begins. Another year, another Season—the ostentation and pageantry; how I abhor such things. He participated more out of obligation than the pursuit of pleasure. Whenever he attended private balls, the eager mamas who paraded their young daughters about disgusted him. He often found himself the unwilling recipient of much of their attentions. Darcy was a strong patron of the theatre, however. He found the occasions to go to the theatre much more to his liking, and he attended often, whenever he was in town, thus, his purpose in being there that evening.

He had been in town for almost a week without an occasion of seeing her. Charles had called upon him at his townhouse, but Darcy had yet to call upon the ladies at Bingley's home. His first occasion to see Elizabeth was afforded when he invited the Bingleys as his guests at the theatre. Darcy was mesmerised by the sight of Elizabeth descending from Bingley's carriage. He was captivated by her in the environs of Hertfordshire. Seeing her now, more elegantly attired in keeping with the latest fashions of Society, he was enthralled. Caroline Bingley was handed down from the carriage next. Upon espying Darcy, she did not wait for him to approach. She made her way forward and attached herself to his arm.

With Caroline clinging to him, Darcy joined the rest of Bingley's party and offered his greetings. At last, Bingley was afforded the occasion to escort his wife to one of the most highly acclaimed performances of the Season. The outpouring of attention Jane and Bingley attracted was a testament to her loveliness. Elizabeth stood apart from the handsomely coupled Hursts. Unable to wrestle himself free of Caroline, Darcy walked toward her.

"Mrs. Calbry. You are a vision." Her warm smile gave him to believe she harboured no ill will against him pursuant to their last meeting. Darcy took it as a good sign. "May I have the honour of escorting you inside?"

"Why, I thank you for the compliment, Mr. Darcy. But you are engaged as an escort, are you not, sir?"

"In such cases as this, I am sure I will be excused for having two such lovely ladies on my arm," he said, remembering to include his clinging appendage in the compliment, as he offered Elizabeth his free arm. The party walked into the theatre, not stopping to engage in conversation with anyone, though many heads turned in their direction and attempts made to garner their attention. Upon entering his luxury box, Darcy assisted the ladies into their seats. He took the seat closest to Elizabeth.

Elizabeth attracted the attention of men and women alike, during the course of the evening. All of them wondered who she was. Although the news of Bingley's marriage was known amongst those who would care to know it, no one was knowledgeable about the newest member of his party. Was she a member of Bingley's family? Was she simply a friend of the family? Was she with Mr. Darcy? Who was this upstart? What were her connections? Such questions swept the theatre during the course of the performance.

After the theatre, Darcy invited everyone back to his home for a late dinner. Elizabeth was impressed with the stateliness of the rooms, the furnishings, and the overall ambience of Darcy's home. She found it exactly as she might have expected of him. She was amused throughout the evening in witnessing Caroline assume a most proprietary air as she moved about the place. That Caroline thought of herself as mistress of the establishment was evidenced by the way she ordered everyone about. The most disconcerting thing from Elizabeth's perspective regarding Caroline's behaviour was Darcy's demeanour. Not only did he not object to Caroline's antics; he ignored her presence entirely. Darcy was interested in only one person that evening—herself!

When the time for his guests to take their leave was approaching, Darcy suffered disappointment as he contemplated the emptiness of his home without her. The first evening spent in Elizabeth's company after many months taught him how much he had missed her teasing wit and her alluring charms. He determined he would do everything in his power to spend time with her over the next weeks. He joined Jane and Elizabeth, who stood together admiring a painting of Georgiana.

"Mrs. Bingley, will you and Mrs. Calbry honour me as my guests on the morrow, assuming you have made no other plans. I wish to introduce you to my sister." The last thing Elizabeth wanted was to meet a miniature incarnation of the man whose penetrating gaze robbed her of her composure, and find in her as acute and unembarrassed an observer as he had ever been.

Jane read in her sister's countenance the nature of her sentiments. "Mr. Darcy, I thank you for your warm invitation. My sister and I shall be delighted to make Miss Darcy's acquaintance. Charles has spoken of her often and with considerable fondness."

"Thank you, Mrs. Bingley."

Caroline approached them and laced her arm through Darcy's. "Mr. Darcy, I need your help in settling a matter with Charles and Louisa." Refusing to broker disappointment, she ushered him to the other side of the room.

"Jane," Elizabeth began once she was satisfied of their privacy, "what were you thinking in accepting Mr. Darcy's invitation on my behalf? You must have known I was on the verge of begging off."

"Indeed, that is why I graciously accepted for both of us. What do you have against poor Mr. Darcy?"

Jane had not believed Wickham's tales of woe regarding Darcy, as she much preferred to believe some sort of misapprehension existed on both parts rather than to think badly of either. Though Elizabeth had repeated every word of Wickham's account of the story to Jane, she had never told Jane of the conversation she had had with Darcy that day in the library. Therefore, she had not related to Jane how she had been a poor judge of character with respect to Mr. Wickham, that she was no longer inclined to believe him.

"Jane, I grant you that Mr. Darcy is a fine gentleman." Elizabeth glanced across the room and confirmed what she suspected. His eyes were fixed on her. "Nonetheless, he is far too officious when it comes to directing my life. You simply do not know him as I do."

"Be that as it may, he is Charles's closest friend. That speaks highly of his character. If your sentiments towards Mr. Darcy have anything to do with your good opinion of Mr. Wickham, I caution you not to allow your regard for him to make you unpleasant in the eyes of a man of ten times his consequence."

Upon their arrival the next day, Darcy introduced Jane and Elizabeth to his sister. Georgiana was fond of Bingley and was delighted to meet his bride. She was curious to meet Elizabeth as well, recalling how her brother had mentioned her on more than one occasion in his letters penned from Netherfield during his sojourn in Hertfordshire.

Mr. Wickham had committed a deception in his description of Miss Darcy as being proud, for the observation of but a few minutes convinced Elizabeth the young lady was only shy. She was less handsome than was her brother, but astuteness and good humour defined her face. An unassuming and gentle nature informed her manners. Elizabeth was much relieved by discerning such differences between the siblings. She liked *this* Darcy.

* * *

Accounts of Bingley's beautiful sister had spread throughout the *ton* by the time of the Bingleys' attendance to their first private ball of the Season. Mrs. Elizabeth Calbry was spoken of as a young widow of exceeding charm and vivaciousness, though in possession of little to no fortune of her own and living at the mercy and benevolence of her younger sister and her husband.

Elizabeth had garnered much attention amongst the gentlemen. Much to Darcy's disappointment, by the time of his arrival, her dance card had filled. Though he despised the idea of dancing in general, he had looked forward to a set with Elizabeth. Instead, he was to stand about the room most of the evening, admiring her from afar, whist she received a steady out-pouring of attention from the gentlemen in the room and looks of carefully concealed disdain from the women.

Darcy hardly lacked his share of attentions, but he was not one to notice. He only had eyes for one person in the room, though he endeavoured to conceal his admiration.

Within days, the Bingleys began to receive a steady stream of callers—some gentlemen, some women—but mostly single gentlemen. Bingley grew concerned, and Jane remained cordial, but Elizabeth showed her delight by treating each caller to her witty repartee and stunning smiles. A normal day at Bingley's townhouse was quickly centring on Elizabeth's social calendar. The callers came from various walks of life—aspiring tradesmen who sought a connection to the Bingleys as their own entrance into the higher circles, wealthy gentry wishing to claim an introduction that would bolster their guest list for balls and dinners, young wives wishing to make an acquaintance with Jane, and older women simply wishing to find out more of the beautiful ladies making the scenes and provoking such gossip.

Soon, the Bingleys received a call from an acquaintance of their relatives in Scarborough ... Sir John Brandon. Sir Brandon's appearance in Bingley's home was met with pleasure. He was silent and grave, and though his face was not handsome, his countenance was sensible. His address was gentleman-like. He was a widower with two daughters, one six and ten years, the other four and ten. They resided on a modest estate in Somersetshire. Elizabeth was drawn to his strong sense of family and honour, though she perceived him as too solemn and even a bit old as he was on the wrong side of forty.

Shortly after the departure of Sir Brandon, Bingley's butler presented a silver salver bearing the card of Lord Felix Winthrop. The gentleman arrived with his aunt, Lady Julia Smithers, whose acquaintance with the Bingleys had resulted from Louisa's marriage to Mr. Hurst.

Her ladyship was elegant, and her countenance was favourable. She was fond of her nephew, who though wealthy in his own right, having inherited his father's title and the estate, was also her sole beneficiary. Six feet tall with broad shoulders and tapered thighs, he was uncommonly handsome. His deep voice was charming and expressive. His manly beauty and more than common gracefulness rendered him exceedingly captivating.

Elizabeth found interest in every circumstance belonging to him, and she met him with the intelligence and wit that defined her. Her frankness and vivacity secured the largest part of his discourse to herself for the rest of his visit.

The leave-taking of Lord Winthrop and his aunt preceded the arrival of a Mr. Horace Cranford and his sister Miss Margaret Cranford. Young people of fortune, he had a large estate in Norfolk, and she had twenty thousand pounds. Miss Cranford had attended the same school as Caroline. Long ago, she had suffered an unrequited fancy for Bingley, and was thus curious to meet the woman who had secured his heart. Her brother, always willing to accompany his sister wherever she might wish to go, did not want to forego the prospect of meeting Bingley's sister-in-law about whom he had heard such tales as to make her an object of his curiosity.

Miss Cranford was remarkably pretty. Her brother, though not handsome, had a certain air and countenance. The manners of both were lively and entertaining. He was delighted with the prospect of knowing Elizabeth better. All accounts of her wit and charm proved true. That day, however, he checked his enthusiasm, preferring to attend the three ladies in equal measure. He did not wish to come off as too bold at the onset, though he fully intended to call again soon, perhaps without his sister.

* * *

Lord Winthrop, having made the acquaintance, took the opportunity to call upon the Bingleys on the following day without his aunt. He made no pretence regarding the purpose of his visit. He wasted no time in taking a place beside Elizabeth. They resumed their conversation on many of the topics they had only touched upon the previous day. By far the most charming and agreeable of any of the gentlemen of her acquaintance, the enthusiasm in Elizabeth's eyes could not be concealed. She believed no subject they might speak on capable of fostering any form of dissension. Weary of the aristocrat's charms, Bingley nudged the fellow on with a somewhat subtle reminder of the morning calling hours having long since ended.

When he had left them, Jane moved to her sister's side and took her hand. "Well Lizzy, have you anything more to discover about Lord Winthrop?"

Elizabeth was certain her enthusiasm for the man's attentions had been unrestrained. She had been excited to learn of their similar tastes in music and poetry, even in books. She schooled her countenance to one more befitting a mature woman. "I am sure I do not take your meaning, dear Jane."

"I am rather sure you do. You have already ascertained the gentleman's opinion in almost every matter of importance, whether it is of books, music or politics. What more will you have to discuss, when next you two meet?"

What was the use in pretending otherwise? Elizabeth was enthralled. She commenced speaking with Jane with much more enthusiasm than she had enjoyed in months. "He is everything a gentleman ought to be!" Guardedness soon etched across her face. "Still, I fear I may have shown too much enthusiasm for such a short acquaintance. Do you not think so?"

"Lizzy, you are excited! You are determined to have fun this Season. What better way to start than in the comfort of your own home? You will have time to curb your enthusiasm once we are amongst strangers."

"I suppose you are correct. However, I have been mistaken in the past. Lord Winthrop has promised to call tomorrow. Please say you will remain with me while I endeavour to learn more of his character, just in case his good looks exceed his good intentions."

"Of course, I will. You must promise to remain by my side, as well, when beautiful young women descend upon my home, feigning an interest in me when in truth it is only to glean information on my dear husband's choice of a wife."

"Why! I believe that is the most unforgiving speech you have ever made. Well done! It would vex me, indeed, if you fell victim to anyone's pretended regard." The two sisters embraced and retreated to Jane's upstairs sitting room to discuss and compare notes on the many morning callers, as was fast becoming their habit.

* * *

Lord Winthrop was a wealthy, handsome man who at nearly one and thirty, had managed to elude the wedding altar for years. Like Darcy, he too had lost his beloved father at an early age. He too was highly sought amongst the young ladies of the *ton*. Except for equally pleasing physical qualities, the similarities ended there. With his agreeable manners, no one dared to accuse him of being haughty and aloof.

Elizabeth encouraged Jane to invite the gentleman to dinner. She insisted Sir Brandon be invited as well, for she had grown fond of his company. Jane was not surprised when Elizabeth asked that Mr. Darcy not be invited, despite his being Bingley's closest friend. Elizabeth tried to convince Jane that Darcy would likely not wish to attend anyway, what with the addition of the Gardiners amongst the dinner guests. Jane had remained unconvinced and had been reluctant to slight anyone, especially one who was held in such high esteem by her husband and herself, for that matter. She broached the subject with Charles and was relieved to learn from him that Darcy had a prior commitment the evening of their dinner party and would not be offended.

Though Caroline and Louisa did not prefer to dine in their brother's home if it meant being in the company of the Gardiners, they made that night an exception. Never had Charles entertained someone of Lord Winthrop's standing. Always eager to advance their own standing amongst the *ton,* what choice had they but to attend? It vexed Caroline that her brother-in-law's connections with Lord Winthrop had been the means of his being introduced to her adversary. Caroline had thought it distasteful enough that Eliza Calbry had captured Mr. Darcy's fancy during those weeks in Hertfordshire.

"Are those fine eyes to cast a spell upon every eligible bachelor who crosses her path?" Caroline often bemoaned to Louisa.

Elizabeth detected Lord Winthrop suffered none of the pretensions she had witnessed in some who were half his rank. She was pleased with his easy acquaintance with her aunt and uncle. Still, with the remembrance of George Wickham's duplicity fresh in her mind, she resolved to remain cautious.

After dinner, Elizabeth was asked to exhibit at the pianoforte, a request to which she readily consented. She completed two songs and garnered everyone's enthusiastic applause, Caroline and Louisa notwithstanding, for her talents. One other guest held back in his praises, as well. Though he was appreciative of her performance and he demonstrated it by his unwavering attention, Sir Brandon said not a word. *He wants nothing save a bit more liveliness in his life.*

The Hursts held a dinner party of their own a few nights later. Darcy attended. Though he suffered no desire to socialise with the Hursts in their home, he was favourably inclined to accept this invitation. It afforded him the opportunity of seeing Elizabeth again. Mr.

Cranford and his sister were also guests that evening. Miss Cranford was delighted to make Darcy's coveted acquaintance, at last. Her brother, he already knew. With Caroline, Louisa, and Miss Cranford vying for his attention, Darcy's time was monopolised. Elizabeth would not have noticed, however. Mr. Cranford agreeably engaged her for the entire evening.

That night, in the comforts of her warm bed, Elizabeth reflected upon the many gentleman callers the Bingleys had received and the new acquaintances she had made. Two of them stood out amongst the rest. What exciting prospects for gaiety during the Season—just as she had imagined. She was resolved to enjoy herself as much as she pleased and flirt with her favourites as much as she dared. She had but one caveat. She would not let her guard down—not yet.

Chapter 8 – Of a peculiar kind

Elizabeth disguised her discomfort with an occasional nod, a knowing smile. A new acquaintance, Mrs. Cecilia Carter, had recently crossed the threshold of matrimony and now found herself the beneficiary of the wise counsel of Mrs. Richmond on the particulars of the marriage bed. Lady Anna Norris, Lady Marie Hargrove, and Jane rounded out the morning callers. *Poor Cecilia.* Elizabeth had no desire to trade places with her.

"You are embarrassed, my dear. You need not be, for you are amongst friends. All totalled, we have over fifty years of experience in managing, shall I say ... over-zealous husbands."

"I daresay some amongst us are quite adept at managing other women's husbands, as well."

Cecilia coughed. Elizabeth coloured. Jane demurred.

"Lady Marie speaks from experience, no doubt."

Lady Marie, a beautiful widow of one and thirty, suffered no offence pursuant to her dear friend's spoken sentiments. "I admit to having enjoyed more than my share of lovers. I might mention most of them represented themselves damned well." Her hazel eyes twinkled in reminiscence. She smirked. "I find no shame in the aforementioned regard. In fact, I would not have it any other way."

Elizabeth and Jane had been no strangers to local gossip over morning tea, but the genteel practices within the confines of Hertfordshire had not prepared them for this. When talk of whose wandering husband was sleeping with whose embittered wife encroached upon the conversation, Jane and Elizabeth wished for the opportunity to disappear into the woodwork. How might they make their escape without affronting their hostess? Sandwiches and cake had not even been served. At last, the serving of refreshments brought a pleasant lull in the conversation as everyone partook of the light repast. Polite small talk did not last long.

"Lady Marie, Lady Anna ... our new friends will make a welcomed addition to our party at Almack's, do you not agree?"

"I have no objections to the scheme; however, *our* new friends are related to tradesmen, are they not?" What Lady Norris lacked in beauty, she made up in strict adherence to society's dictates. She always spoke freely on such matters, regardless the audience.

"Oh, yes. I do recall having heard something along those lines." Mrs. Richmond face matched the crimson flowers in the vase atop her mantle.

"What a shame," Lady Anna said. "The prospect of you ladies joining us would have made for a refreshing change. However, I do not make the rules."

"How shall we ever recover from *our* disappointment?" Elizabeth asked with impertinence.

Endeavouring to leave the indelicate topic behind, Mrs. Richmond spoke candidly on another. "Have you set your cap upon a particular gentleman to accompany you as you embark upon your foray out of widow's weeds?"

"I beg your pardon?"

"Mrs. Calbry, need I speak more plainly? You are a beautiful woman. Please say you do not intend to hide yourself away, when the Season offers such titillating prospects for adventure."

Seeing Elizabeth's embarrassment, the older woman said, "Do not mind me, my dear; I am only teasing. But mind you, when you do decide to jump back into the fray—in a manner of speaking—I wager many charming gentlemen are waiting in the wings, any of whom will do the job admirably."

Lady Marie, renowned for her independence and vivaciousness, took a keen interest in Elizabeth. She discerned in her a kindred spirit, both having been widowed at a young age. However, she had been fortunate in having married an earl. He had spoilt her exceedingly during his life and had graciously provided an ample settlement for her upon his death. A merry widow indeed! She had her own money. She had power and freedom. Above all, she controlled her own destiny.

Jane excused herself, stating her desire to refresh herself before taking her leave. Lady Marie took advantage of Jane's absence to speak with Elizabeth.

"I confess to having heard of you long before today. I am delighted to have had a chance to talk with you this morning. You are the most delightful creature to grace our presence in years. I wish to take you under my wing, to *sponsor* you amongst the *ton*, in a manner of speaking, both you and your lovely sister. I shall call on you in a day or so."

Meanwhile, Caroline and Louisa paid Miss Cranford a morning call. Ever an astute observer of anyone she perceived as a competitor for Darcy's affections, Caroline had not failed to notice the lady's attentions to Darcy at the recent dinner party.

"I was delighted to observe you and Mr. Darcy getting along so famously last evening. One's affianced and one's closest friends must be amiable."

"What on earth are you speaking of, Caroline? Mr. Darcy gave no indication of being engaged to anyone."

"Oh yes, dear Margaret!" Caroline exclaimed. "He and I are quite attached to each other."

"You do not say. May I ask if this attachment is of a long duration? I have read no notice in the paper. I have heard no talk of it. Is the gentleman even aware of its existence?"

"Our engagement is of a peculiar kind. However, few beyond our intimate circle have wind of this. Therefore, I must beg for your utmost secrecy."

Louisa sat nearby in astonishment with thoughts of a similar bent as those of Miss Cranford. *When will my poor sister realise her pursuit of Mr. Darcy is a hopeless cause? I am more likely to secure his affections than she is. How Caroline manages to convince herself of a chance with the gentleman is beyond comprehension.*

The next day, Miss Cranford included a visit with the Bingleys in her morning calls. Though she did not believe a word of Caroline's declaration, she decided to discover what she might, nonetheless.

"Mrs. Bingley, Mrs. Calbry, it is a pleasure to see you this morning."

"Indeed, I am delighted you called. My sister and I had hoped to call on you by now. You will forgive us our tardiness?"

"Think nothing of it. In fact, one of my purposes in visiting is to extend an apology on behalf of my dear brother for his neglect. He, too, wished to be here. Alas, he was called out of town for a few days to visit his friend in the country."

"I pray all is well with your brother's friend, and he shall return to town soon."

"I assure you, Mrs. Calbry, everything is quite well."

"When do you expect his return?"

"My brother will return in a week. We should like to invite you and your sister to be our guests at dinner soon thereafter."

Miss Cranford was delighted when the butler announced Mr. Darcy. Upon his entrance, the gentleman made a poor attempt in hiding the fact his gaze was irresistibly drawn to Elizabeth, and only Elizabeth.

"Mrs. Bingley, I am here to see Charles. Is he about?"

"Charles has gone out. However, I expect his return any minute. You are welcome to partake of tea with us, while you wait."

"I am much obliged." His eyes directed towards Elizabeth, although, try as he might, he was unable to discern Elizabeth's sentiments.

"Mr. Darcy, you do remember Miss Cranford."

"Yes, of course. It is a pleasure seeing you again." Darcy bowed slightly. "Mrs. Calbry, it is a pleasure seeing you, as well. How are you this morning?" Darcy took a seat beside Elizabeth and remained there throughout the visit.

Upon taking her leave, Miss Cranford could not help wondering about Darcy's behaviour. His assertion he had called upon his friend no longer proved convincing. His gaze always returned to Mrs. Calbry, whenever he was not engaged in conversation with Jane or her.

Does something exist between those two? Although she scoffed at any possible competition coming from Caroline Bingley's quarter, this presented a different scenario—one she had not envisioned. Her unsuspecting brother might have competition. Miss Cranford determined to write to her brother at once to implore him to finish his business in the country forthwith, and return immediately to town. She considered they both might be of some use to each other.

* * *

Gentlemen spent much of their time at their clubs for one reason or another, not the least of which was to talk of the latest gossip. Thus, when word of a young widow gracing the scenes amongst the social circuit reached Darcy's hearing, he wanted to find out more.

The rumour being circulated at White's described the lady as beautiful, alluring, charming, and witty. Some remembered her late husband, Mr. Daniel Calbry of Hertfordshire, for his womanising proclivities. Surely, the dear lady must be in want of companionship, someone to warm her bed on lonesome nights. A wager had been placed on White's betting book as to who would be the happy partner in that endeavour. That wagers were commonly placed upon any and everything was no secret. The discovery that the widely accepted practice had marked Elizabeth as the object of derision for the entertainment of these gentlemen rendered him ill.

Had this been the reason for the over-abundance of attention she garnered from those men when she had attended the ball the night before? He had noticed he was just one of several gentlemen in awe of her that night. Hearing of the wager persuaded him that the preponderance of attentions paid to her might have been by design. Darcy resolved to do whatever he must to protect Elizabeth from ignominy merely for sport.

* * *

Elizabeth interrupted her writing and stood upon his abrupt entrance. "Mr. Darcy, this is a surprise. Two visits in the course of one day. Charles is not here; he and Jane are out." She took her seat and gestured for him to do likewise.

"No." He waved off her invitation to sit. "I am here to speak with you on a matter of grave importance ... in privacy." Darcy flexed his fingers nervously. How was he to embark upon such a delicate discourse?

"What have you to say that requires privacy?"

"Mrs. Calbry, no doubt you garnered considerable admiration during the ball, last evening."

"I shall not argue your point, sir. You also enjoyed considerable admiration from the young ladies and their mamas. I wonder you took the time to pay attention to my activities."

When had he ever occupied the same room with her with his eyes drawn elsewhere?

"You understand the difference, I trust. Whereas I might receive as much admiration as will be bestowed upon me and even delight in it, a similar reception on your part would cast you in a negative light."

"I object to your insinuation, sir. Is it my fault I am admired?" Elizabeth responded flippantly.

"I grant you, Mrs. Calbry, your charms are hard to suppress, but you might remember that a woman in your situation should not expect to receive those flatteries normally bestowed upon young maidens in the same vein as when bestowed upon a beautiful young widow." He drew nearer and took a seat beside her.

"Do you mean to give offence? What are you suggesting, Mr. Darcy?"

"Mrs. Calbry, do not pretend to miss my meaning. You know of what I speak. If you do not, then I encourage you to guard your attentions to gentlemen with far more circumspection than you do."

"I do not take your meaning, sir! What business is any of this to you? Unless, of course, you are simply jealous." Elizabeth surmised she was on to something. "Mr. Darcy, you are jealous because I do not receive your attentions with as much pleasure as you might wish."

"Jealous?" His face revealed righteous indignation. "You do flatter yourself, Mrs. Calbry. As you are aware, I admire and respect you, and due to that respect, I will not stand by and allow those who do not have your best interests at heart to take advantage of you."

"Perhaps, you view the matter as such, but I prefer to believe otherwise. You, sir, are jealous and rather insecure, I might add. It vexes you to witness me attracting the attention of older, more experienced gentlemen than yourself."

"You are dreadfully naïve! What does my age have to do with my desire to protect your reputation?"

"Why everything! However, I suppose one must be older and more experienced, as are the other gentlemen of my acquaintance, to appreciate the many nuances of relationships amongst those of the opposite sex."

"In this case, I wish you would take my words to heart and not dismiss them because of your lack of understanding of my *experience.*" Darcy stood to take leave of her company. He neatly bowed. "Good day, Mrs. Calbry."

Darcy left with the firm belief that Elizabeth would believe nothing he said. He would have to go about the business of protecting her more covertly; otherwise, she might suppose he was interfering in her life yet again, as she had supposed while in Hertfordshire.

Elizabeth threw up her hands in frustration. *Good riddance!* Who would not be flattered by the attention she was receiving? The last weeks had been akin to the time before her forced marriage when she had enjoyed her maidenhood with nary a care in the world.

How dare he suggest I am naïve? He comprehends nothing of my situation. He barely looks at a woman—except me. I refuse to allow that dour man to dampen my spirits.

Hours later, Elizabeth had yet to put the argument with Darcy behind her.

The arrogant Mr. Darcy is jealous! Imagine that. She would make him even more jealous as retribution for his presumptuousness and heavy-handed treatment.

Chapter 9 – Such another man

Horace Cranford was quick to heed his sister's plea to return to town, even though he was agreeably engaged in the pursuit of a young woman on the verge of surrendering to his irresistible charms. He reckoned this lady friend, along with the rest of his paramours, must wait, for he endeavoured to put his sister's wishes before everything else, such was his devotion to her. It had been his way since the tragic loss of their parents a decade past and such it would remain.

The morning's warm sun erased any signs of the downpour from the night before, rendering the day perfect for the afternoon outing. The bright gowns worn by the ladies rivalled the yellows, pinks, and violets of the sweet-smelling blossoms that landscaped the garden paths. Cranford accompanied his sister. The Bingleys attended, as did Darcy. Cranford and Darcy were far from strangers. Both were members of White's, and they had had many opportunities to socialise with each other over the years, yet little camaraderie existed between them. Had it not been for his sister, the same would be true of that day. With Margaret on his arm, he approached Darcy and Bingley.

"Pleasure seeing you, Bingley! My sister shared the happy news of your family's acceptance of our invitation to dine with us in my home this week. We look forward to the evening with delight."

"Indeed, it is a pleasure for us to accept. I assure you Mrs. Bingley and Mrs. Calbry look forward to it, as well."

"Capital. Might I ask if Mrs. Calbry is about?"

"Indeed, she is. I believe she is in the house."

"Then if you will pardon me, I will seek her company forthwith," he said and turned to his sister. "Margaret, my dear, I shall leave you in the capable hands of these fine gentlemen."

"I should not mind one bit. I am certain I am safe. What say you, Mr. Darcy?" She laced her arm through his and moved closer. Bingley took the hint and plotted his retreat.

"By all means," Darcy answered distractedly. He would be more than happy to remain with Miss Cranford for a spell, and then deliver her back to her wayward brother when he espied him with Elizabeth.

Across the lawn, Caroline panicked! Why was Mr. Darcy speaking intimately with Miss Cranford?

"Mr. Darcy! I have been searching all over for you," she cried, gasping for breath, having run the length of the lawn.

"And so you have found me, Miss Bingley. What do you want?" he asked in a tone far harsher than he had ever used with her. Her alarm heightened. Had Margaret spoken to him of the "secret" attachment?

"Join me inside. I wish to show you something."

"You fail to appreciate that I am speaking with Miss Cranford. Can it not wait?" There! He spotted Cranford and Elizabeth coming out of the house, arm in arm. "Please excuse us, Miss Bingley." He coaxed Miss Cranford to walk with him, and they made way towards the house. To his chagrin, he lost sight of Elizabeth amongst the sea of parasols.

Relief etched across Darcy's face when Elizabeth emerged from a path with Bingley and Jane some quarter of an hour later. Best of all ... no Horace Cranford. Sensing an opportune moment to re-join his friend, Darcy bid Miss Cranford adieu with a light kiss to the back of her hand. Caroline, who had been hovering close by, was shocked by the appalling display!

Mr. Cranford, having left the company of Mrs. Calbry, was quick to locate his sister. "My dear sister, I am afraid you have used me most ill. I wish I had remained in the country; I assure you, my lady suffers no tender regard for Darcy," Cranford decried upon approaching Margaret.

"And how did you reach such a conclusion, dear brother?"

"I dare not tell you all my secrets," he offered. "But what say you? Did I not do well in placing you in Darcy's way? Have you any success to divulge?"

"I shall not complain. He can be charming and amiable. Save a pointless interruption by Caroline Bingley, I was the happy recipient of his ardent attention for the past half hour." Margaret would have to have been as daft as was Caroline to suppose she held Darcy's undivided attentions. "Nevertheless, I am more and more convinced he is far more interested in *your lady* than he would wish for anyone to discern."

"Who would not be?"

"Perhaps, you! I see no lasting advantage in your forming an attachment to Mrs. Calbry." In fact, she was decidedly against his forming any sort of serious regard for the lady. She knew her brother well. She did not wish that he should maltreat Elizabeth or subject her to derision; she merely wanted her removed as a competitor for Darcy's affections.

* * *

True to her word, Lady Marie called upon Jane and Elizabeth within days. She even remained with them until the last callers had taken their leave. After Lady Marie had also departed, Jane and Elizabeth discussed the bevy of morning callers, specifically her ladyship.

"Jane, Lady Marie is such an amazing woman. Never have I met someone who exemplifies the much-acclaimed attributes of a truly accomplished woman, and added to all this she is independent; she decides her own fate without deferring to any man. Extraordinary!"

"What do you say about her own admission of wantonness? She expresses no regret in that regard."

"I shall not judge her. What some regard as wantonness might just as well be deemed an expression of liberation ... a celebration of independence. Her late husband, the earl, died years ago. Why should she be miserable? Why should she not enjoy the freedom afforded by her tragedy?"

Jane dismissed the chills along her arms with a certainty that her sister spoke merely in jest. "Do you not think she will ever remarry, Lizzy?"

"I certainly do not, for she as much as told me so. To do so, would be to hand her fate, her independence, her fortune, everything ... to the control of another. I must say not only do I admire her steadfastness, but I also am rather inclined to agree with her."

"Do you mean to say you do not hope to remarry one day?"

"I assure you, dear Jane, I shall never remarry. My fortune of a few thousand pounds, as small a sum as it may be, is mine, and I shall not hand it, along with my freedom, to any man. I shall not find myself at anyone's mercy again."

Jane knew not how to respond to her sister's declaration. "What is a fortune of any size without someone to share it with? I imagine Lady Marie is rather lonely."

"Oh Jane, not everyone can be as blissful as you and Charles. I do not begrudge you one moment of happiness. You are such a good person; you deserve it more than anyone."

"I count my blessing each night for my marriage to such a good and amiable man. Dearest Lizzy, how I long to see you as happy! I wish for such another man for you!"

"Jane, do not cry for me. I assure you, I do not intend to make myself unhappy about my situation. I relish my freedom."

Days later at a private party in Mayfair, Elizabeth and Lord Winthrop found themselves in each other's company once again. He arrived late and greeted the lady of the house before securing a comfortable spot from which to admire the woman whose presence was his sole reason for even attending that night.

"Mrs. Calbry, I was beginning to fear I might never get a chance to secure you to myself."

"Lord Winthrop, you are selfish, are you not?"

"Not the least bit, my lady. Did I not wait patiently for the past half hour for you to extricate yourself from your boring companion?"

"Lord Winthrop, if you are referring to Sir Brandon, I assure you, my lord, he is not the least bit boring."

"If you insist, madam." Lord Winthrop raised Elizabeth's hand to his lips and imparted a light kiss. "Nevertheless, you do not receive Sir Brandon's attentions with the level of unbounded enthusiasm as you do mine. Why do you think that is?"

Elizabeth's smile confirmed his assertion. She did appreciate Sir Brandon. Despite his gravity and reserve, she beheld in him an object of interest to herself, a sort of kindred spirit. His reticence was not from any gloominess of nature, but rather from disappointment of hopes.

She often considered how he must still suffer the loss of his wife, while bearing the trials of raising two daughters on the cusp of maturity. Elizabeth's compassionate nature would surely make the gentleman an object of her respect, as well as her pity.

How in the world might one compare such a man of silence to one as lively as Lord Winthrop?

"You need not answer this instant. With you now by my side, I shall endeavour to keep you here for the rest of the evening."

The aristocrat's deep voice had interrupted her reverie. "Lord Winthrop, if it is constancy in a companion you seek, I wonder you do not marry to secure a lasting convenience of that kind."

"Perhaps I have yet to meet a worthy lady ... or perhaps I have, and the lady would not have me. Did you ever consider I might suffer an unrequited love? Perchance, I might be nursing a broken heart. Now, here *you* are. If I give my heart to you, will it be safe?"

"Lord Winthrop, let me assure you, it is not your heart that I seek." Elizabeth spoke the words honestly, not wishing to increase his expectations ... but the manner in which she spoke the words excited the gentleman's hope.

"Plainer words have never been spoken, madam." He placed a lingering kiss upon her hand.

Hours later, Elizabeth sat alone with Lady Marie in an upstairs sitting room.

"So, Elizabeth, you have had ample time to get to know Lord Winthrop. Tell me at once, what do you think of him?"

"I find him everything of worth and amiability."

"Surely you are aware he is smitten with you. He is completely in your power!"

"You are far too generous in your estimation of my sway over the gentleman. I like him, I dare not deny, and I delight in his attentions. I am satisfied to leave it at that," Elizabeth affirmed.

"Who am I to contest, if that is how you truly feel? However, I suggest that if you hesitate to secure him, he will move on. He is a man with a prodigious ... shall I say ... appetite. Patience is not his forte."

Elizabeth knew not what to say. What did she care should Lord Winthrop abandon his pursuit? He was a worthy conquest, no doubt, but she was not out to capture anyone. Charming and being charmed in return, for no other reason than the pursuit of fun, described Elizabeth's intent. *How might her ladyship perceive such frivolity?*

At length, she responded, "I appreciate your advice, Lady Marie, and I shall consider it."

* * *

The number of private balls, theatre outings, dinner parties, and soirees on the Bingleys' social calendar was nowhere near letting up as the Season progressed. Elizabeth readied herself with considerable care for the evening's dinner party. To her dismay, none of her favourite suitors was in attendance upon her arrival. She missed Lord Winthrop's company the most, their recent *tête-à-tête*, notwithstanding. Though she had made it clear to him that she was not interested in forming a serious attachment, he did not relent in his attentions towards her. If anything, he became even more attentive, his constancy convincing her of the depth of his worth as a true friend.

"Are you looking for anyone in particular, my dear?" Mrs. Blakely, the hostess of the evening's festivities, tapped Elizabeth's shoulder to garner her attention. "Mrs. Calbry?"

Elizabeth coloured. She had been staring at the door throughout the evening. "Pardon me?"

"I asked if you are expecting anyone in particular."

"No." Elizabeth lied. The truth was she looked towards Lord Winthrop's arrival with immense enthusiasm. *He promised he would come. Where is he?* She had counted upon his being there to spirit her away from the tiresome pastime of sitting with married women, widows, and confirmed spinsters, who watched the merriment from the corner of the room. If any of the women thought anything of her liveliness of spirit when in his company, they spoke not a word of it ... in her hearing. Lord Winthrop was considered a brilliant catch for any woman, and many mothers with eligible daughters did not intend to give up hope, despite his ardent attentions to the beautiful young widow.

A quiet hush pierced the room. Someone whose acquaintance Elizabeth had not yet made entered. She was a young woman of no more than seven or eight and twenty. Her face was handsome. Her figure was tall and striking, and her address was graceful. Elizabeth was more than a little taken aback upon her subsequent discovery. The elegant late arrival's escort was none other than Mr. Darcy, his face bearing none of the discomfort she ascribed to him when in the company of Caroline Bingley.

His manly beauty and more than common gracefulness combined with her arresting beauty and defined elegance made it possible that, in all of England, a more striking couple would not be beheld. Elizabeth found it difficult to direct her attention elsewhere; such was the state of her busy imagination.

Who is this beauty on Mr. Darcy's arm? When has he ever been as contented in a lady's presence?

From across the room, she watched as Darcy introduced his lady companion to Jane and Charles. As Elizabeth observed Darcy's attentiveness to the striking beauty who remained by his side, she began to reconsider her scheme to make the gentleman jealous, and she began to think that perhaps she was mistaken about him after all. His pleasing demeanour towards the lady caused Elizabeth to consider that only intimacy made it so.

Why have I never seen this side of Mr. Darcy before? Elizabeth wondered what other secrets the enigmatic man harboured.

Chapter 10 – In want of a wife

The evening did not end soon enough to suit Elizabeth. *Mr. Darcy's companion indeed held him in raptures throughout the evening. He never once looked at me!* Elizabeth's thoughts were aflutter during the carriage ride home. She could wait no longer to question Jane.

"Who was the beautiful creature attached to Mr. Darcy's arm this evening?"

"Dearest Lizzy, did Mr. Darcy neglect to introduce the two of you? She is his cousin!"

"SHE is his cousin? Miss Anne de Bourgh?" *Mr. Collins's description did not do the lady justice. She is the woman whom he plans to marry.* She sat back against her seat in stunned silence.

"No, Lizzy. Lady Victoria Middleton, the former Lady Victoria Fitzwilliam. Mr. Darcy escorted her tonight because her husband was detained. She did not wish to miss the Blakely's soiree."

Elizabeth had no idea what to think of any of this. In retrospection, she might convince herself of her complete indifference. *Is Mr. Darcy engaged in some sort of subterfuge to incite feelings in me, which are not to be borne?*

Every day, for the next few days, proved good ones to Elizabeth's way of thinking. She and Darcy had suffered little of each other's society. She had decided he indeed was trying to provoke in her feelings of jealousy by arriving at the dinner party with his beautiful cousin attached to his arm, heightening the mystery by avoiding her throughout the evening, hence foregoing an introduction, which would have settled her active imagination.

He, on the other hand, was growing frustrated by her profound stubbornness in heeding his advice to guard her behaviour more circumspectly.

The following evening, the Bingleys attended another private dinner party. Darcy was amongst the guests, as well as many of his long-time acquaintances, including Lady Marie Hargrove and Lord Winthrop. Lord Winthrop was making no secret of his admiration of Elizabeth. Darcy was troubled witnessing how much the two of them delighted in each other's company.

Darcy cornered Bingley as he made way to the card room.

"What is the situation between Mrs. Calbry and Lord Winthrop?"

"Do not get yourself in a state, Darcy."

"A state? This comes as a complete surprise. When did they become such intimate acquaintances?"

"Lord Winthrop has visited Elizabeth in my home. He is a decent fellow, is he not?"

"How long has this been going on? Does he often come around?"

"Darcy, I hesitate to get into the details of the comings and goings of my sister's acquaintances. Suffice it to say, Lord Winthrop is but one of many steady callers."

When Elizabeth was not delighting in the charms of Lord Winthrop, Darcy noticed she had garnered the attention of Lady Marie. His thoughts exploded.

* * *

The incomparable Lady Marie Hargrove and the elusive Mr. Darcy knew each other quite well. Described as a woman who controlled her own destiny, she was beautiful, vivacious, charming, and clever; it was no secret she had an appetite for younger men. Her late husband, Lord Winston Hargrove, was her senior by several decades. She had married him at the tender age of seventeen, when he was in his late fifties. Throughout the marriage, he had been aware of her sexual proclivities. He had not cared. He had adored her, and while his eldest son inherited the bulk of his estate, he had meant to make certain Lady Marie should never want for anything.

When Darcy had first become acquainted with her ladyship, it was not with the intention of engaging in a long, torrid affair ... far from anything of the sort. He was as repelled by her unrelenting attentions as he was by those of the young ladies of the *ton* and their aggressive mamas.

Lady Marie was cunning and had more resources to bring to bear in the pursuit of a young man than the typical conventional young maiden had at her disposal. Though at least seven years his senior, she was blessed with an alluring blend of exquisiteness and charisma which combined to make her almost impossible for any man to resist.

Darcy, not yet two and twenty at the time, had recently suffered the loss of his father. His initial appearances in Society after the conclusion of his official period of mourning had encouraged a consensus that a young man of his status must be in want of a wife.

He suffered relentless pursuit as ambitious mothers paraded their daughters before him as prospective brides. Darcy was not looking for a wife, as Lady Marie was able to discern. She had approached Darcy with something different in mind. The prospect of a no strings attached romantic liaison was better suited to her purposes, yet it was not enough to tempt Darcy. He stood firm in his strong sense of right and wrong.

Darcy returned to his townhouse in a rush one fateful afternoon. He had hurried home to dress for dinner with his uncle and aunt, Lord and Lady Matlock, whom he had not seen in weeks. The door of his apartment was ajar.

"Good, you are here, Yves," Darcy said as he pushed the door open. Walking inside, loosening his cravat, he continued, "I will wear the black getup tonight, and hurry. I am running behind schedule. My aunt will have my—Lady Marie!" The enticing seductress lay upon his bed in all her breath-taking beauty, as naked as God had created her.

She rose from the bed and took him by the hand. Her perfume overwhelmed his senses. His treacherous body's reaction was discordant with his pending speech. She then placed a silencing finger on his lips.

"Do not talk." She had made the healthy young man an offer he no longer wished to refuse.

Lady Marie was ravenous. Widowed for less than two years, she relished the status she enjoyed in having been married to an earl for over a decade. Her generous inheritance provided her with her own lifetime establishment in the highly fashionable Mayfair. Over the course of time, Darcy became as familiar with her townhouse as he was with his own.

She demanded proficiency in her lovers, and Darcy did not disappoint. He soon proved as sensual and deft as she imagined he would be during the many months of her pursuit. As promised, Lady Marie made no demands upon Darcy other than that he share her bed ... at least in the beginning. In due course, she began to make requests of him with increasing alacrity. Lady Marie was living far too extravagantly and exceeding her income. She had insinuated as much to Darcy.

Her inheritance was more than adequate for a sensible woman. With such generous terms, she had little chance of destitution, especially if she exercised even the slightest economy. Her touted role dictated she dared not to, should she risk losing her coveted position amongst Society.

Darcy began to question her saneness when she accused him of treating her as nothing more than a mistress after relentlessly pursuing her. As his mistress, she should be compensated accordingly. Furthermore, she insisted the two of them must be seen in Society in each other's company, other than as mere acquaintances. The liaison, proffered as no strings attached, had become a noose around his neck, and Darcy began to acquit himself from her clutches. He ended the relationship amidst the lady's violent protests of being ill-used.

* * *

Darcy learned from Bingley later that evening that Lady Marie had called upon Elizabeth at their townhouse. The two had become fast friends. Lady Marie's intention to pursue a friendship with Elizabeth caused Darcy some degree of concern. No one held more steadfast to the distinctions between rank and privilege than did she. She had expressed her disdain for Charles Bingley on more than one occasion to Darcy, for no other reason than his family's fortune having been acquired in trade. He wondered what she was about.

The next evening was the occasion of the much-anticipated Howards' ball. Everyone who was anyone was, therefore, to attend. Elizabeth was intent upon keeping her distance from Darcy, perceiving him as more and more obsessed with her each day, to the extent of his being jealous, not only of the attentions she received from men, but also of those received from women, as well. Darcy called on Elizabeth at the Bingleys' early that day.

At her invitation, they took their seats in the drawing room.

"If you are here to see my brother, I fear you have missed him again, or perhaps you are aware he is not at home, and you simply chose this as a convenient time to upbraid me on my recent conduct," she said saucily.

"Mrs. Calbry, your powers of perception do not fail you, I see, when it comes to construing my motives. I rather wish you would exercise those same powers when it comes to some of your newer acquaintances."

"Speak plainly, Mr. Darcy. What have you to warn me of now?"

"Though you are disinclined to believe I have your best interests at heart, I shall persist in my admonitions. I would not wish to render you suspicious of society in general, but you should be aware of some situations."

"For instance, Mr. Darcy?" Elizabeth implored. Her impatience with Darcy threatened any semblance of civility.

"How acquainted are you with Lady Marie Hargrove?"

Her astonishment reflected on her face! "Mr. Darcy, do not presume to ask questions of me, the answers to which can be of no concern to you."

"Anything that affects you is of concern to me. You are Bingley's sister, and he is my closest friend. What do you know of the lady?"

"I know she is kind. There are many similarities in our lives. I enjoy her company immensely. There. Are you quite satisfied?"

"I suppose your assertions will suffice for now. Nevertheless, I know Lady Hargrove quite well. I do not believe the two of you have anything in common."

"That is not for you to say! If you will excuse me, I must prepare for this evening's ball. Good day, Mr. Darcy." Elizabeth abruptly stood and quit the room, leaving Darcy sitting there alone—speechless.

* * *

There was little wonder why Darcy did not request Elizabeth's hand for a set that evening. He was annoyed with her beyond measure. He did not even endeavour to keep Elizabeth in his sight. Another woman consumed his thoughts. He espied *her* as she sat at a table with Elizabeth. Darcy did not hesitate to approach the two of them. He acknowledged Elizabeth with the slightest of bows, but he extended his hand to Lady Marie. Without uttering a single word, he led her to the dance floor and took his place opposite her.

A discernible astonishment swept throughout the ballroom. However, no one was more astounded than the lady herself, no one except Elizabeth. She had seen the two of them in the same social setting before.

When did they become so—familiar? Elizabeth witnessed the fearsome woman whom she had come to regard as a mentor of sorts, submit to Darcy's silent command, as would a young schoolgirl.

"Mr. Darcy," she said at length, having fully recovered from the initial shock and endeavouring to gain some sort of advantage, "to what do I owe the honour of this dance? Have you realised no other woman can warm your bed as exemplarily as I once did?"

"I would not say that, Lady Marie."

"Then what do you say? Or are we to go through the entire dance without a word between us?"

"I am curious. You have never been supportive of Charles Bingley, yet I understand you have called upon his sister several times," he responded after a long pause.

"Of what concern is any of this to you? Surely, Elizabeth Calbry is not your current lover, for how can she be? It is no secret Lord Winthrop has designs on her."

"Of course *you* would think that is where my interest tends. However, in light of how you have always found any association with Bingley insupportable, the fact that you pursue a friendship with his sister gives me pause."

"Fear not; I like her. I do not hold her brother's connections to trade against the lady herself. To get to the true point of your concern, I shall not disclose the nature of our *friendship* to her," she ventured to say as they drew together once more.

"I am not afraid of you, Lady Marie. I simply question your motives. If you maintain your motives are sincere, I can have nothing more to say on the matter." Darcy's tone indeed insisted he would speak no more, and he thereby remained silent throughout the remainder of the set, despite her many attempts to engage him in conversation.

Endeavouring to take Lady Marie at her word and put the matter out of his mind, Darcy stood outside on the balcony for a few moments of solitude after supper. He soon discovered he was not alone. Another couple had sought refuge on the balcony, in what they supposed was a secluded spot. Darcy recognised the gentleman as Lord Winthrop. The woman, he could not make out as her companion shielded any view of her. Darcy moved to a more advantageous spot.

Chapter 11 – Till this moment

His bruising grip upon her arms sent tremors down her spine. What was she thinking in agreeing to meet him alone? They most assuredly would be detected if he did not lower his voice.

"I have dedicated the better part of the Season to this scheme. I cannot be expected to wait much longer!"

Her bravado fled in the wake of his brusque manner. "Unhand me at once, you brute!" Her voice trembled. "You realise this is neither the time nor place for this discussion."

He tightened his grip. "I am running out of patience! I compensated you amply to deliver her to me."

"These things take time. It is taking longer than I thought to gain her trust. Her self-righteous sister accompanies her wherever she goes. We have scarcely a moment alone together."

"I shall not continue to wait forever to get what I want. I will expect the return of every pound I have advanced to you if I am forced to take matters into my own hands!"

"Such threats are unnecessary. I promise it will be soon. She has agreed to meet me in my home for an afternoon of tea and conversation. We only need to settle a date. I am just as anxious as you to get this over with. Do you think I enjoy being in company with these people?"

Darcy had heard enough. He was appalled!

* * *

Elizabeth was admitted into the blue salon.

"Mrs. Calbry, my mistress expresses her regret for her delay. You are welcomed to wait here until her return. I expect her arrival any moment."

Elizabeth walked about the ostentatious room. Her eyebrow arched. She lifted and scrutinised delicate figurines whilst she waited and took care to return them where she had found them. Having satisfied her mind on the matter of her ladyship's peculiar taste—after all, who expected nude figures on a mantle?—she soon settled into a chair, one, unfortunately for her, designed more for spectacle than comfort. Moments later, the butler opened the double doors and in walked another guest.

"Mrs. Calbry, how lovely to see you!"

Standing to offer her hand and receive the compliment of the light kiss he bestowed thereupon, she smiled. "Indeed, it is a pleasure, Lord Winthrop."

Elizabeth took her seat. "We are both to wait for her ladyship. I expect she will arrive soon."

"Indeed. Though, I should not place too much reliance on her imminent arrival, my dear Elizabeth."

His sudden familiarity caught her by surprise. Elizabeth endeavoured to remain unruffled, now in recognition of the impropriety of her situation should Lady Marie be detained much longer. Even her increasing regard for Lord Winthrop did not find her wishing for time alone in his company.

"I am certain I do not comprehend your meaning, my lord. Lady Marie persisted in requesting my attendance this afternoon. She surely would have informed me had she expected not to keep the engagement." At least Elizabeth hoped as much.

"Our dear friend, Lady Marie, has been gracious enough to allow us use of her home for as long as we choose. This way we can be discreet." He moved away from Elizabeth to walk to the door of the drawing room. He turned the key. The sound was faint in comparison to her exploding heartbeat.

"Sir, you assume too much. I do not wish to spend time alone with you!" She rose from her seat and walked towards the fireplace, eyeing the hearth, the mantle, for anything she might use in protection against him, should matters take a perilous turn.

Lord Winthrop positioned himself in front of the fireplace, directly in her path. "Elizabeth, this is no time to feign modesty. I have seen the way you look at me and how you have accepted my attentions in turn. You have long been wishing for the opportunity to give yourself to me. Your desire for me is as urgent as is my desire for you," he said with deep yearning whilst drawing ever nearer to her, his mind intent upon achieving his goal. He was convinced she was toying with him. He was not opposed to playing rough, should she wish it.

"No, my lord. I fear you have misread my sentiments." Her voice trembled with trepidation.

"Have I?" He now stood before her and traced his finger along her neckline. "Have you not responded to my teasing challenges, tit-for-tat, with saucy repartee and evocative innuendos, and tormented me mercilessly with your alluring wit? You have shown me through your coquettish conduct how much you want this. I do not mean to leave here until I am thus fully satisfied." He stood even closer to Elizabeth with the intention of placing his hands upon her arms and engulfing her in a passionate embrace, truly believing her a frustrated woman, desirous of his affections. He leaned forward to kiss her lips, but Elizabeth quickly ducked and escaped to another part of the room. He followed her, cornered her, and hovered over her. He stood as close to her as possible—his warmth chilling her body.

"You have perfectly misunderstood my intentions." She had mastered her voice, but her eyes conveyed her fear. "Did I not make it clear to you, Lord Winthrop? I have no greater desire than mutual friendship between us."

"Indeed, you made your intentions abundantly clear, madam, as you well know." His breath seared her face as his eyes focused on hers. "This will happen today. You and I have courted this moment all Season." He whispered, his lips close to her ear, "We can do this nicely or not so nicely. I much prefer the former."

Astonishment that a man she had learned to trust would behave in such a manner, gave way to alarm in finding herself in such a precarious situation. She felt vulnerable, manipulated, betrayed, hopeless, and lost. *If he dares to touch me, what shall I do? Scream? Who would come?*

Lady Marie has contrived this whole scheme! What kind of wo-man would subject another to such a harrowing fate?

Why had she befriended me at all—only to betray my trust in her? Cast into such a powerless state, she found her predicament too incredible to believe.

A faint sound interrupted the rapid pounding of her heart. Both Lord Winthrop and Elizabeth looked towards the door—one in silent indignation, the other in gratefulness for deliverance.

Darcy entered the drawing room, imperturbably, and approached the two of them. Offering the temptation of a handsome reward as an inducement, he had made private arrangements with Lady Marie's butler to inform him at once when Lord Winthrop came around.

Startled because Darcy had entered the room without disturbance through the door he had made certain to lock, Lord Winthrop demonstrated calmness he did not possess. "Good afternoon, Darcy. This is a surprise indeed. I might ask if Lady Marie is expecting you. Then again, when did you ever require an invitation to visit the lady?"

"I might ask the same of you, Lord Winthrop." Darcy turned his attention towards Elizabeth. She had seized the chance to move away from Winthrop. Her countenance spoke of her anguish and embarrassment. He bowed. "Mrs. Calbry, this is a welcome surprise indeed. You look uneasy. Am I interrupting anything?"

"No—not at all, sir. I am happy to see you! I had planned to meet Lady Marie, but she is detained. Would you be so kind as to escort me to my brother's home—at once? I find I can no longer wait to leave this place."

"Mrs. Calbry, I would be most honoured if you will allow me to escort you. We should continue this conversation, and it seems Darcy is here to call on Lady Marie."

"Mrs. Calbry has expressed a desire to leave. I am at her disposal, I assure you," Darcy stated resolutely, not even favouring Lord Winthrop with a glance, his eyes reassuringly fixed upon Elizabeth.

"Mrs. Calbry, I insist you allow *me* to escort you home. We are not quite finished here."

"Indeed you are wrong, Lord Winthrop. I have said all I wish to say to you. Nothing more remains to be discussed." The uneasiness in her voice belied her calm demeanour.

Lord Winthrop was enraged, but he did not intend to create a scene. Darcy did not mean to back down; Lord Winthrop read it in his stance. He relaxed his clenched fist. "This is all well and good. The satisfaction of winning a bloody wager is not worth all this aggravation. This has been a complete waste of my time. I gladly take leave of you, madam." He stormed out of the room and out of the house with a loud slam of the front door.

Humiliated, Elizabeth collapsed in a chair and buried her face in her hands. Her brush with what would have been a traumatic and devastating experience had ended. Darcy rushed to Elizabeth and knelt on the floor before her. Taking her hands in his, he looked into her eyes— once lively, now filled with despair.

"Mrs. Calbry, is everything all right? Did he harm you?"

"No, I am relieved to say he did not. Thank Heaven you arrived when you did. Notwithstanding, how did you know to come? What on earth did he mean by a wager?" Elizabeth begged to know, relieved, but rather bewildered by her fortuitous reversal of fortune.

Darcy bestowed a grateful kiss upon her hands. "I would prefer we did not talk here. I want to explain everything to your satisfaction. Allow me to escort you to my home, where we can speak in privacy. I must apologise, for my sister is away. However, I will send word as soon as possible for Bingley and your sister to join us for dinner."

* * *

A widow she may have been ... even a witty, impertinent one, but Darcy found it disquieting to have the discussion he knew he must have with Elizabeth, whom he regarded as having the sensibilities of a maiden. Once they settled in his drawing room, and he was satisfied she was beyond the initial shock of her encounter with Winthrop, and indeed ready to talk, he took a seat beside her and began.

"Mrs. Calbry, you are a beautiful and charming woman," he tentatively began. "I am afraid a commonly held belief exists that women whose situations are not unlike yours," here he paused and considered his next words before he cautiously continued, "having been 'introduced' to physical relations in the marriage bed ..." Darcy tugged at his cravat. Why did he find this so difficult? At length, he continued, "... are eager to resume said activities as soon as can be."

Elizabeth, uncharacteristically, had not uttered a single word. He did not fail to notice her discomfort. He decided at that moment that he must tell her the whole account.

"Combine said sentiments with the propensity of gentlemen to make sport of any and everything—the long and short of the matter is a wager was placed at White's on who would be the first to seduce you."

It took a moment for his words to register with her. Comprehension slowly etched on her countenance. Elizabeth coloured. She sought to hide her face in her hands in shame, but Darcy stopped her by resting his hand upon hers, while he lifted her chin with his free hand.

"I am sorry to have to tell you this, to be the one to inform you that you have been the target of such maliciousness on the part of those who are, ironically, called gentlemen. Perhaps, I might have come right out and told you from the start, but I daresay you would not have believed me. It is a cruel and abhorrent sport and not something you, I, or anyone might have prevented or controlled."

Elizabeth reflected upon his statement. "The one thing I might have controlled, I suppose, is my behaviour; instead, I was most unguarded in my attentions, with Lord Winthrop more than others.

"He accused me of misleading him. I cannot say I blame him for thinking as he does. I am grateful you arrived when you did. Did you suspect something nefarious was afoot? How did you know?"

They continued their candid discussion on the events leading up to that afternoon. Elizabeth's sensibilities altered between resentment and mortification as Darcy described how he had questioned the sincerity of Lady Hargrove's motives, based upon their past association; how his suspicions were confirmed when he overheard Lady Marie and Lord Winthrop plotting against her, and how he took matters into his own hands to thwart their plans.

"I suppose I might be a bit angry with you for not being more forthcoming with me in your reproaches. I know you tried to warn me, many times. I am only angry with myself for refusing to listen.

"I am most obligated to you, Mr. Darcy. How shall I ever repay you?"

"Let us not speak of it. As Bingley's sister and, dare I say, as a dear friend, I am obliged to do everything in my power to protect you."

"I consider it a deep debt. I must find a means of thanking you properly."

"If you insist, Mrs. Calbry, perhaps in time."

"I must beg your indulgence in one other respect. I beseech you, Mr. Darcy, say nothing of this unfortunate incident to my brother. I should hate for him to think he needs to defend my honour and place all of us, especially my sister Jane, in an uncertain state. Allow me to learn from this mistake."

"Yes, of course. I would do almost anything you ask of me." He rested his hand upon hers.

"How shall I put an end to the malicious speculation? What can be done to settle the wager and close the books on the sordid affair forever?"

"The gentleman's honour is engaged. No one would dare lay false claim to it. You need not worry on that account. As difficult as it may be to suppose, these things are commonplace at the club. Interest will fade. In time, this shall pass. I promise you."

"But I do not like having the matter linger, forever serving as an insult to my integrity. Perhaps *you* might lay claim to the wager."

"I cannot do such a thing. I suppose I might be flattered that you would even consider such a scheme," he said soberly, hoping that she would recognise the gravity of her statement while endeavouring not to chastise. "However, I would not dishonour you or Bingley in that way. This shall pass. You must trust me on this."

"What other choice is there?" Elizabeth stood, retreated towards the window, and stared out in silence. Darcy wished there was something he might do to help. Decorum necessitated he respect the boundaries of their tenuous affiliation.

After a while, Elizabeth said, "Mr. Darcy, if you do not mind, I would like some time alone to refresh myself before Charles and Jane arrive for dinner."

"Of course, take as much time as you need. My staff will prepare a room for you at once."

Alone in the well-appointed room, Elizabeth reflected upon her trying afternoon. She thought of how Darcy had come to her rescue, had treated her with the utmost care, and had not judged nor berated her for her incautious behaviour. She lay upon the soft bed hoping for a brief nap, anything that would calm her restless mind. Sleep would not come, there was to be no immediate respite from her foolish actions.

The events of the afternoon had shaken her more than she cared to admit. Her salvation—she owed it to Mr. Darcy. Despite months of abusing him abominably to his face, he had treated her with kindness, gentleness, and patience. Recalling the moment that he lifted her face to his, what she discerned was not a man with an expression of accusation nor was it one of pity. She detected in his eyes as much pain as she felt in her heart. Tears on her part would surely have been met with his own. Though he might not hold the incident against her, she would not let herself off so easily.

She was ashamed. Of neither Darcy nor Lord Winthrop could she think, without realising she had been blind, partial, prejudiced, and absurd.

I behaved despicably. For months, I courted preconceived opinions and ignorance—driving reason away at every turn, finding pleasure with the preference of the pretentious and suffering offence by the officiousness of the deserving. Until this moment, I never knew myself.

As Darcy remained downstairs in his library awaiting the arrival of his guests for dinner, he also indulged in a great deal of thought of the events of the afternoon. Grateful he had intervened on her behalf before it was too late, he was also encouraged that Elizabeth was beginning to accept that he had only her best interests at heart over these past months. He was making progress in his quest to pursue Elizabeth. He had begun to gain her trust.

The evening proved the most pleasurable occasion the four of them had yet shared in town. Bingley was pleased because Darcy and Elizabeth managed the entire evening without a single quarrel. When he implored Elizabeth to perform on the pianoforte, she found his request impossible to refuse. Darcy, mindful of her attempt to put on a bright face despite the trying events of the day, moved across the room swiftly to attend Elizabeth and offered to turn the pages for her as she performed.

As the opportunity presented itself, he spoke to her softly, "You are exhausted. Perhaps we should end the evening after this performance. I think it is best you get some rest. Do you not agree?"

Elizabeth's weary smile signalled her concurrence. Their private exchange did not go undetected. Jane was delighted to observe Darcy and Elizabeth behaving cordially towards each other, for she had always held Darcy in high esteem. Still, she did not fail to discern at times throughout the evening her sister's spirits waned, particularly when they had separated from the gentlemen after dinner. She wondered what had happened to cause such a change in her sister's attitude, and what if any bearing existed to justify Elizabeth's presence at the Darcy townhouse when her original destination had been Lady Marie's home.

Jane suspected her sister had much to tell, the only question in her mind being when she would share it.

Chapter 12 – Improved in essentials

Darcy had not mentioned a word of the incident at Lady Marie's to Bingley, as promised. Elizabeth was much obliged. She was determined to learn from her mistakes. Elizabeth's courage always rose with any attempt to intimidate her; this would be no exception. Although she did not withdraw from Society altogether, she scrutinised her outings with greater care. She guarded her attention to gentleman acquaintances cautiously. She regarded Lady Marie Hargrove with feigned courtesies whenever their paths crossed. When others deigned to remark that Lord Winthrop had transferred his attentions elsewhere, she smiled with unaffected pleasure and expressed her profound wishes for providence befitting his character.

It was the Bingleys' turn to have the Cranfords for dinner. Elizabeth had grown weary of Mr. Cranford's attentions, suspecting, but not knowing, he had an interest in the wager.

"Jane, I realise it is only fitting that the Cranfords should join us for dinner. However, I have no desire for company this evening. Would you be terribly upset if I begged off for the evening?"

"Lizzy, you insisted upon returning the favour of a dinner party to the Cranfords. Therefore, you are obliged to attend. Besides, is Mr. Cranford not one of your favourites?"

"Jane, it is complicated. I find I hardly know who my true friends are anymore."

Jane stopped what she was doing and went to her sister's side. Her angelic eyes filled with concern; she placed her hand upon Elizabeth's hand. "Whatever do you mean? Has something happened?"

Elizabeth smiled. "Oh! Never mind, dearest Jane. Of course, I shall attend tonight's dinner party with the Cranfords."

Jane thought of Elizabeth's evasiveness in trying to explain her change of attitude and wondered more than once about Elizabeth's dampening enthusiasm towards the Season's gaiety—first Lady Marie, then Lord Winthrop, and now Mr. Cranford. One by one, Elizabeth eschewed the same people whose company she heretofore had enjoyed the most. Jane, herself, was beginning to grow weary of the arduous social demands. She surmised Elizabeth was, as well.

Mr. Cranford had observed Elizabeth most of the evening without a chance to engage her directly. The perfect chance came when Caroline began to perform at the pianoforte. Elizabeth sat off to the farthest side of the room alone. He approached her with no doubt of the eagerness of her reception. He was surprised by her lukewarm greeting, especially having witnessed no such lack of enthusiasm for anyone else at the party, including Darcy. Cranford had paid attention throughout the evening to how Elizabeth and Darcy looked upon each other far more favourably on that night than he ever recalled of their previous encounters. Darcy was solicitous towards her, and she was pleasantly amenable.

"Mrs. Calbry, it is a pleasure to have a few moments to speak with you discretely. Forgive me for my neglect," he spoke in a hushed voice so as not to distract from the musical entertainment.

"Mr. Cranford, having greeted each other at the start of the evening was pleasant enough. I assure you, sir, I have not felt the least bit neglected," she replied, speaking as softly as he did.

"Then, perhaps I suffer neglect in not having my share of attention from the most beautiful woman in the room." He reached for her hand, a gesture she tactfully declined.

"Allow me to thank you for the compliment; however, such adulations are unnecessary. I am aware of your opinion on my beauty, for you have missed no opportunity to broach the topic in the past. When you and I speak of anything henceforward, let us discuss books, music, or even the weather. I have thought better of our past dialogues and since found I have no desire for sugared flattery."

Cranford cast a pointed eye in his *new* rival's direction. "Can this change of heart have anything to do with your newly-found regard for Darcy?"

"I am sure I do not take your meaning, sir."

"In the past, you have made no secret you did not value him, yet the two of you spoke at length throughout dinner in a manner which could be interpreted as intimate."

"I have always appreciated his worth as a gentleman. Having allowed myself to know him better, I think Mr. Darcy improves upon acquaintance."

"Indeed!" Cranford's dubious glare did not escape her. "Pray tell," he started, but checking himself, added a gayer tone, "Is it in address that he improves? Has he deigned to add civility to his style? For I dare not hope," he continued in a lower and more serious tone, "that he is improved in essentials."

"Oh, no! In essentials, I believe, he is very much what he ever was. However, in knowing him better, his disposition is better understood."

A lady stands before me, who has clearly transferred her affections to another and is no longer enamoured of my charms, he composedly considered. Although he would have been more than content to leave it at that, he owed it to his sister to distract Elizabeth's attentions from Darcy; he had promised her that he would do that and no more.

"What of the talk of his engagement to Miss Bingley; does it not concern you?" he asked in an even more hushed tone.

"I am aware of no such talk, but as you obviously are, does it not concern you that your own sister is enamoured of Mr. Darcy? She does not attempt to conceal it. Perhaps she would benefit more from any speeches you have in regard to his *engagement*."

"I will endeavour to counsel her, but while I am speaking with you at this moment, I urge you to know what you are about."

"I have no wish for disingenuousness with you, Mr. Cranford. Allow me to speak candidly. You and I have no true basis for you to express such concerns on my behalf. Only you can speak to your true motives, but as I suspect they are in complete contrast with my own, I ask you to refrain from any further discussion with me on such matters."

"As you wish, Mrs. Calbry, please accept my apology for any effrontery. It was unintended."

Their discourse thus at an end, he bowed, and then removed himself to the opposite side of the room to join his sister. She was eager to know what had transpired with Elizabeth. Now perceiving Elizabeth as a true threat, she welcomed her brother's aid in keeping her away from Mr. Darcy.

"So, dear brother, what have you learnt?"

"I am afraid I can no longer be of any assistance to you, dear sister. Though the lady has not professed an undying love for Darcy, she has certainly made her feelings for me clear, and I have far too many willing conquests to concern myself over the one who got away," he asserted, more aggrieved over disappointing Miss Cranford than any lingering blow to his ego.

"Horace! How can you give up?"

"Easily—I suggest you do the same. In fact, I am off to the country in three days hence. I shall expect you to accompany me!"

* * *

Darcy was now counted amongst the regular callers at the Bingleys' home, with the added advantage of being able to do so at just about any time of day or evening. Not a day had passed since the afternoon at Lady Marie's, that Elizabeth and he did not spend at least two hours in each other's company. He favoured late afternoons, often missing Bingley and Jane and enjoying Elizabeth's exclusive audience. He always managed to miss Caroline and Louisa whenever he called, as well. How he accomplished such a feat, Elizabeth had no idea, but that it was not merely coincidence, she had no doubt.

They began to explore their common interest in reading and Darcy encouraged Elizabeth to borrow as many books from his library as she desired. He often came bearing books of his own choosing, and the two would spend time in Bingley's library reading and debating. This was in no way reminiscent of former times at Netherfield Park, however, for Caroline Bingley was not fawning for Darcy's attentions, and because they genuinely respected each other's views, neither was inclined to argue opinions not entirely their own, purely for the sake of challenging each other.

Darcy entered the drawing room on one afternoon, expecting to greet no one but Elizabeth, only to find someone whom he had not previously met, keeping her company. Mrs. Gardiner had chosen that day to pay a long-overdue visit to her nieces. Elizabeth had not expected the afternoon to go well at all—not that she lacked confidence in her aunt's social acumen, but because she did not know how Darcy would receive her London relative after his initial exposure to her Hertford-shire relations. She was pleasantly surprised to observe how amiable Darcy could be, when he chose to put himself forward.

When the discovery was made that Mrs. Gardiner and Darcy shared an interest in the town of Lambton, just a few miles away from Pemberley, the two spent the greater part of an hour in animated dis-cussion of the charms of the village.

Once Darcy had left the Bingleys', Mrs. Gardiner remarked to Elizabeth on his behaviour.

"Lizzy, he is not at all as you described him earlier this year. Why did you say he was haughty and ill-mannered?" Mrs. Gardiner asked. "I witnessed nothing of the sort. He has no semblance of ill nature. On the contrary, he bears something of dignity in his countenance that would not give one an unfavourable idea of his heart."

Her esteemed aunt's praise of him increased Elizabeth's new-found approbation of Mr. Darcy. She was obliged to admit she had misjudged him and since learnt to appreciate him more as a true friend. Hearing this made Jane happy. She had appreciated, first-hand, how impressed Darcy had been with Elizabeth for some time.

Days passed. The more time Elizabeth and Darcy spent together, the greater became her regard for him. So much so, Elizabeth started to toy with the idea they might be something other than friends. As she began to consider her circumstances as a young widow and how it had affected people's perceptions and expectations, she considered that those same expectations might prove somewhat liberating once care-fully considered—sexually voracious women, having been introduced to the pleasures of the flesh by their late husbands, dolorous widows perpetually in want of a male companion.

The mere thought of Mr. Darcy incited pleasant but unfamiliar feelings in Elizabeth. Passionate stirrings she had theretofore never known conspired with her increasing regard for the gentleman, leaving her longing for his daily visits, spending as much time in his sole com-pany as propriety allowed.

With no intention to remarry, she had few choices—an existence devoid of true passion or a romantic liaison with a handsome, thoughtful, and desirable man. The latter being the case, only one man would do; she was certain of that. Should she ever deign to take a lover, then it must be Mr. Darcy. The more she thought upon it, the more her interest awakened.

"Mrs. Calbry, the weather is pleasant this afternoon. Will you join me for a carriage ride in Hyde Park?"

"I think not, Mr. Darcy. I have no desire for society at this time. I much prefer to remain indoors."

"Can this be the same woman I met in Hertfordshire—the same woman who could hardly be restrained from venturing out of doors?" he asked undeterred, endeavouring to persuade her to his way of thinking.

"Yes, but one can hardly compare the solitude of a walk in Hertfordshire to the spectacle of a carriage ride in Hyde Park during the height of the Season."

"Please, consider my invitation, if only for a short while to have a change in scenery and to enjoy a breath of fresh air. What would be the harm?"

"Are you not concerned with giving rise to gossip and speculation over the nature of our alliance, should we be seen together?"

"No—I am not. If you are concerned, then come to my townhouse instead. I have a rather nice garden you have yet to see. Everything is beautiful at this time of the year. The gardens are acclaimed for their beauty. Let us spend the afternoon at my home. Georgiana is there. She will enjoy seeing you again."

"If you insist." She was eager to spend the afternoon with him, in an intimate situation.

"I insist!" Darcy beamed with delight over his triumph.

It was indeed a pleasant outing. Georgiana and Mrs. Annesley remained with Darcy and Elizabeth in the garden until the tea service was removed, at which point they left the two to their own devices.

Darcy and Elizabeth had begun spending so much time together he believed himself quite adept at reading her moods. He recalled one particular afternoon when her inattentiveness had led to her defeat in three consecutive chess matches. Darcy enjoyed winning, but not like that. Their most recent afternoons together had proved no better as regarded her mental acuity. Gone were the hours spent debating philosophy and world religions. He began to worry she had not fully recovered from the encounter with Lord Winthrop or perhaps she simply had had enough of Society.

"How are you today, Mrs. Calbry?" he asked, attempting to interrupt her from her reverie.

"Oh, I do not know. I am poor company this afternoon, I admit. I am afraid I have much on my mind," she said as she continued her pensive manner.

"You look melancholy. Has something happened to steal your joy?"

"No—some days are not always as good as others. I suppose this is one such day."

"I know just the thing to revive your spirits!"

"Oh and what is that, Mr. Darcy?"

"Come to Pemberley."

"To Pemberley?" she repeated in wonderment. "I am certain that Charles and Jane will be glad to accept your invitation. However, I suppose, I should return to Hertfordshire. In fact, I think I should like to return as soon as can be. I have had enough of town to last for quite a while."

"I should not think they would want you to return to Hertfordshire without them. You would enjoy Pemberley, I dare say, as much as Hertfordshire, even though that is your home. The change will do you good."

"What about your sister? How will she regard an influx of guests?"

"Georgiana has grown rather fond of her cousin in Kent. She will be travelling there with Mrs. Annesley. I will journey to Rosings Park to bring her back to Pemberley at summer's end." Darcy smiled at his triumph. What other excuse might she have? "You see, it will be quite an intimate little party."

"Did you forget to mention the Hursts and Miss Bingley? Are they invited as well?"

"No, although I suspect they may pay a visit at Pemberley upon their return from visiting their relations in the north, but that would be weeks away. I should like it if you will accept my invitation. I know it will do you some good. Besides, you owe me," he teased. "This is the only restitution I will accept."

Elizabeth was ambivalent about the prospect of sharing the better part of the summer at Pemberley with Darcy. She was growing more and more attracted to him while he was satisfied with their budding friendship—platonic, innocent. Each encounter left her incomplete, wanting. He was certainly unlike any other man she had met. Though every good-bye was accompanied by a light kiss upon her hand, which caused her to quiver inside, having spent hours alone with him over the past weeks, the most she had come to expect during those times was an incidental brush on her hand and an occasional touching of arms when he sat closely by her side.

Yet, he must suffer the attraction as strongly as I do. Perhaps his attachment to his cousin, Miss Anne de Bourgh, holds him paralysed.

Having appointed himself my protector, I suppose he does not wish to mislead me. Elizabeth's silent reflection continued. *For goodness sake, it is not as though I wish to marry him! He is quite safe in that respect, for I have no thoughts of matrimony, ever again.*

Should I tell him?

Elizabeth continued to think of the upcoming trip to Pemberley, the possibilities. The summer in Derbyshire with Mr. Darcy—an intriguing prospect, indeed!

Chapter 13 – The handsomest woman of my acquaintance

As if it were not unfortunate enough that the Hursts and Caroline Bingley descended upon Pemberley within days of the arrival of Darcy and his party of "invited" guests, the Bingley sisters came with aggrieved attitudes, determined to vent their displeasure in being excluded from the original group. Why should they not be invited? They were more a part of Bingley's family than the upstart Eliza Calbry.

Having spent precious little time in Darcy's company during the Season, they had no doubts everything would be set right once everyone was invited to Derbyshire. Caroline and Louisa refused to believe Charles when he said only Jane, Elizabeth, and he had been invited. That bit of information only heightened Caroline's disturbance. She refused to believe she had lost her power over Darcy. Poor Caroline! Even she would admit, if pressed, that the gentleman did nothing to encourage her, but he did nothing to discourage her—that was encouragement enough for her!

It had also not failed her notice that Darcy and Elizabeth had grown far more amiable to each other towards the end of the Season—another development she had not seen coming when first they had arrived in town. When exactly had it happened? The last she had heard, Eliza Calbry had captured the fancy of Lord Winthrop, a vexation in itself but far better that she should attach herself to *him* than Mr. Darcy, in Caroline's estimation.

The assemblage of everyone at Pemberley hearkened memories of days at Netherfield Park—Darcy fascinated with Eliza Calbry, only now she was an eager recipient of his attentions. Caroline singled out Darcy after dinner on the first night of her arrival.

"Mr. Darcy, pray tell how your lady finds her future home? No doubt, she loves Pemberley. I dare say even she would be impressed with its splendour," she uttered, her voice teaming with sarcasm.

"Pemberley is favourably received by everyone who visits."

"I wonder what grand alterations she envisions for the appeasement of your dear future mother-in-law. If Mrs. Bennet's schemes for Netherfield are an indication, the transformation of Pemberley promises a marvellous spectacle."

"It would certainly be the Mistress of Pemberley's prerogative to make any changes she deems necessary for her own comfort, as well as that of her family."

"Indeed. Such a fortunate lady she is. And to think, the talk of the Season was over Eliza Calbry and Lord Winthrop." Darcy's serene countenance belied his annoyance.

"I was concerned your fair lady had tossed you aside for a pretty face. How did you bear it?" Caroline beseeched.

"Rumour also has it that you are the future Mistress of Pemberley ... which goes to show you should not believe everything you hear," he said with a sharp reproachful tone.

Teasing man! Caroline refused to give up her jealousy-ridden censorship of Elizabeth. "Eliza is altered indeed. I imagine she suffers the loss of Lord Winthrop's society profoundly."

Despite how much Mr. Darcy disliked such an address, he contented himself by coolly replying that he perceived no such alteration.

Undeterred, Caroline opined, "I never comprehended what the excitement was about—that Lord Winthrop should find her so captivating." Caroline eyed her adversary engaged in quiet whispers with Jane.

"For my own part, I never saw any beauty in her. I do not like her eyes. They are hardly alluring but rather shrewish looking." Caroline perceived no danger in her discourse, and so she continued her unflattering description of Elizabeth's many fine attributes. Determined to provoke Darcy to speak, she continued, "Then again, she charmed you, as well. I believe you thought her rather pretty at one time."

"Yes," replied Darcy, unable to contain himself any longer, "but that was when I first knew her. In all the months since then, I have come to consider that I have never seen another woman who is more handsome."

He then went away, and Miss Bingley was left with the satisfaction of having forced him to say what gave no one any pain but herself. Would she ever learn?

* * *

Though they had been at Pemberley for over a week, Darcy scarcely had the amount of time that he would have wished to spend with his guests. After being away from Pemberley for such a prolonged period, some matters could no longer be deferred nor addressed by the steward.

The little time he spent with Elizabeth was always passed in the company of others, a circumstance that annoyed him. Sending his uninvited guests away would have been indecorous, despite the great inconvenience to himself, and his plans to enjoy the early summer with Elizabeth. As he had expected, Charles and Jane enjoyed each other's company far too much to bother with anyone else. No matter where he turned, he would encounter either Caroline or Louisa, usually both.

One early morning, Darcy had the good fortune of finding Elizabeth in the breakfast room alone. He settled himself beside her and took her hand in his. After imparting a light kiss, he cradled her small hand in his.

"Do you know how much I have missed you? I promised you an intimate party, yet we are beset by two of your least favourite people in all of England."

"What an unforgiving speech, Mr. Darcy."

"You do not deny it. How can I make amends?"

"I am not the least bit disturbed by their presence, I assure you. I am enjoying a delightful time. I revel in the beautiful grounds of Pemberley. Never have I seen a place for which nature has done more, or where natural beauty has been so little counteracted by an awkward taste."

"That means everything coming from you. Your good opinion is rarely bestowed." Darcy partook of the light meal the servant placed on the table before him—scones and piping hot coffee, his usual breakfast fare.

"I am pleased that you are so delighted with my home."

"I am! Pemberley is splendid!"

Darcy responded to her praise optimistically, "But you have yet to see it through my eyes."

"What are you suggesting, Mr. Darcy?"

"Take a walk with me," he urged, "just the two of us. We must leave immediately, mind you; a moment's delay and Miss Bingley or Mrs. Hurst might decide we need chaperons."

Darcy and Elizabeth, agreeing it was for the best, set off soon after their meal. Their journey brought them, after some time, in a descent amongst hanging woods, to the edge of a river. Elizabeth longed to explore its windings, and Darcy was pleased to oblige her, endeavouring to increase their time together as long as possible.

While wandering on in this slow manner, Elizabeth's admiration of the beauty of it all could hardly be contained, but having exhausted the words "delightful," and "charming," in her commendations, she fancied that praise of Pemberley from her might be mischievously construed. Such praises ceased, but her enthusiasm was impossible to subdue.

Having reached his intended destination, Darcy beckoned Elizabeth to sit with him for a brief respite before returning to the manor house. Their view was marvellous.

"Thank you for affording me such a pleasing prospect of your home. I should not have missed it for the world."

"The pleasure is all mine. I thought you might like it here. I believe it is one of my favourite spots in all of Pemberley."

"How fortunate for me that it is such an easy walking distance," Elizabeth said, adding hopefully, "perhaps we might return here soon. A picnic would be nice."

"I should like that very much!"

They walked along, side by side, Darcy with his hands clasped behind his back, Elizabeth with her hands clutched together in front of her. They spoke not a word. Neither of the two wished to impose on the agreeable silence.

The glorious tranquillity was soon interrupted, for just ahead of their path, Caroline waited on their approach. She placed herself between them and attached herself to Darcy's arm. Darcy promptly turned and took Elizabeth by the hand, insisting she take his free arm and even resting his hand over hers. Despite the unwelcome intrusion of a third party, with his hand over Elizabeth's hand resting against his chest, Darcy favoured Elizabeth with an exulting smile suggesting she was the only woman in the world.

Days later, Darcy rode out early to inspect some of his lands. Upon his return, he encountered Elizabeth on one of her solitary rambles about the park. He dismounted his horse and handed it off to his accompanying groom, having decided to walk with Elizabeth, instead of continuing his own venture.

"Good morning, Mrs. Calbry. I see that you remain an early riser."

"Yes, indeed. I find it perfectly tranquil here, and I enjoy a solitary walk," she said, wounding Darcy with the possibility that she did not desire his presence. Elizabeth guessed as much. "Not that I mind your company, Mr. Darcy. I welcome it."

Indeed she did, for Elizabeth had long wanted to broach a particular subject with him, and try as she might, she had not found the courage. The fact that she was unable to bring herself to speak candidly with Darcy vexed her, for she was sure she could speak to him on any subject with impunity. After walking along, neither of them speaking for some time, she broke the silence.

"Pray tell, Mr. Darcy, what was the nature of your association with Lady Hargrove?"

The puzzled expression that crossed Darcy's face at her impertinent question added fuel to her courage. "Come now, Mr. Darcy. You and I both know we will get nowhere if you insist upon treating me as an innocent."

"Have you any doubt on the nature of our past association?" The tension felt moments earlier eased. Perhaps she was not as naïve about such matters as he had assumed, after all.

Elizabeth, having raised the subject at last, would not accept such an evasive response. "So, you were lovers—in the truest sense of the word?"

"Not at all, for I did not love her," he stated technically.

"Did you not like her or even esteem her?"

In response to his silence, she said, "So, it was merely physical. Would you say that men in general are open to such an arrangement?"

"Certainly not always—as you well know having been in a loving relationship yourself."

To that response, Elizabeth's countenance showed an air of confusion. *Why should he assume such a thing?* She thought about it. *Oh, because I have pretended it as so.*

"Am I wrong, Mrs. Calbry?" Darcy asked in witnessing her curious regard.

Should I disclose the truth to him? What would he think? "No, not at all. You are quite right, Mr. Darcy." She decided now was not the time to confess her deeply held secrets, not to Mr. Darcy, not to anyone. Still she was fascinated to know more about his liaison with Lady Hargrove, and though reluctant, he was not wholly disinclined to discuss it.

"In your case, you did not love nor esteem her ladyship, yet you shared such ... such intimacy with her. Why did you do it?"

"I suppose it was something we both thought we needed at the time."

"You *both* needed ... so, you think it is natural that a woman should desire passion as much as a man," she stated tentatively.

He paused to look into Elizabeth's eyes. "Of course it is. To where do these questions tend?"

Elizabeth hesitated. "Never mind me, Mr. Darcy. I am just thinking."

"Thinking what?"

"Oh look, Miss Bingley is just ahead. Let us join her!" Elizabeth said, catching sight of the ever-present Caroline, allowing her no time to respond to his question, and leaving Darcy's mind in a state of utter confusion and astonishment.

Surely, she is not thinking what I think she is thinking!

* * *

Later, way past midnight, Darcy was awakened by the presence of an unexpected visitor in his room. She had waited until late into the night when she was certain everyone else in the household was sound asleep and made her way to his chambers. Dressed in a sheer nightgown, she was about to crawl into his bed, when the slight ruffle of his covers stirred him.

Alarmed and apprehensive, he sat up! "What on earth are you doing here?"

"Is it not apparent? I have seen your looks and witnessed your growing discomfort for weeks. You are noticeably longing for female company." She pulled the covers back to an astounding view of his impressive arousal.

Darcy caught her hand. "You forget yourself, madam. I have no desire for this!" He shifted his position to afford himself greater privacy.

"Your body betrays you." She extended her free hand towards his torso. Darcy second-guessed his penchant for sleeping in the nude. He grabbed the bed cloth and wrapped it about his waist as he got out of bed.

"Return to your own room and do not trespass upon me in this manner again!"

"You mean to say you are rejecting me!"

"Spare yourself, please. Show some dignity. I am willing to overlook this intrusion this once, but should you persist, I will know how to act."

"You must find me desirable!"

"Desirable? I assure you, I have no intention of entangling myself with a married woman, much less the married sister of my closest friend!"

"You have no aversion, whatsoever, to entangling yourself with the *widowed* sister of your closest friend!"

"I beg your pardon, madam. You have no idea of what you speak, and I object to your insinuations." He had reached the end of his patience. "In deference to your husband, your brother, and even your sister, please leave this room at once!

"Devise whatever excuse you deem suitable and leave Pemberley as soon as can be. You are no longer gladly received in my home!"

Darcy locked his door upon her reluctant exit and returned to his bed, as angered as ever by such a blatant invasion of his privacy.

He woke the next morning with the unwavering belief that what he thought had transpired the night before could not possibly have taken place. He reckoned it was a dream—no, not just a dream, a nightmare! Whatever he had eaten the night before, he determined to speak with his housekeeper so that it might never be repeated on the menu. Thus resolved, he sought to put the disturbing dream out of his mind as he drank his coffee and skimmed the paper.

Upon hearing from his housekeeper, at the end of his meal that the Hurst party was preparing for an imminent departure from Pemberley Darcy narrowly averted losing his breakfast.

Chapter 14 – A man who had felt less

The first month of their stay had gone, and the second was under way. A cloud had been lifted from Pemberley with the exodus of the uninvited Hurst party. Darcy had found it ironic listening to Bingley explaining the circumstances of the Hursts' precipitous departure. His account sounded so sensible as to cause Darcy to consider that he may have dreamt the awful incident after all. Best not to dwell upon it, Darcy reasoned. The unwanted guests had taken their leave—little else mattered.

Elizabeth was happy with the circumstances—in some respects, at least. Darcy and she enjoyed far more time alone than they had with Caroline always underfoot, which was a good thing. To her disappointment, she had made no progress in her design to move the relationship beyond their self-acknowledged status as dear friends. Darcy was behaving every bit the consummate gentleman with but one exception.

One afternoon, while sitting alone with her in the library, far too distracted by her nearness to concentrate on his book, Darcy raised a subject with Elizabeth, which owing to its delicate nature, he had put off for weeks.

"As we are now close friends, please give me leave to address you by your given name ... Elizabeth. I mean you no disrespect—it is just that ... you must admit we have grown as close as two people can be over the past months. Must we continue standing on such formality?"

Her immediate thought centred on how they might be much closer. She forced the brazen thoughts to the back of her mind. "I understand, I suppose I might allow such a liberty, but only in privacy, mind you; otherwise, people would assume we are more intimate than we indeed are. You would not want that, would you, Mr. Darcy?"

Darcy considered if she only knew what he wanted—more than anything, he loved her. He wanted to make her his wife. Addressing the woman whom he loved by another man's surname was painful, even a dead man whose memory she cherished. What he needed was more time to determine where her heart was. If asked, would she accept him? Was she ready to move beyond her past? Her understanding of his lack of desire to address her by her surname boded well, he considered.

Of course, she understood; she could not stand being addressed as *Mrs. Calbry* ... not by her closest acquaintances, not by him. His desire to ignore social strictures and address her by her given name boded well, she considered.

One day, Darcy encountered Elizabeth on the way out the door. "Good morning, Elizabeth. Where are you off to with such excitement?"

"I have decided to walk to Lambton this morning."

"I beg your pardon—*walk* to Lambton? From Pemberley?" *How could she even entertain such a notion?*

"Why does that surprise you, Mr. Darcy? I enjoy few things more than walking."

"Be that as it may, it is not appropriate that you should even consider such an endeavour."

Elizabeth gave him a look—one she thought might restore him to his senses. "Mr. Darcy, though I answer to no one," she began, "I might appreciate your counsel, if it were offered respectfully. You speak to me as if I am a child."

"Excuse my manner, Mrs. Calbry. I voice my will to my own satisfaction. As you are the only person of my acquaintance who takes umbrage, I will endeavour to change my tone to one that is less commanding when I speak with you. Does that meet with your approval?" He said the words she professed a desire to hear, but the way he said them did nothing to lend them any credence.

"I imagine it is a small consolation," she derided. *So now I am back to being 'Mrs. Calbry'... that did not take long.*

"I cannot help insisting upon having my way in this. You know nothing of these parts," he expressed out of deep concern.

"I am sure it must be quite safe to journey to Lambton from Pemberley by foot, Mr. Darcy."

"It is always best to err on the side of caution, Mrs. Calbry."

"I think I should be quite safe."

"But what would the local villagers and neighbouring gentry think knowing a guest of Pemberley is scampering afoot about the countryside?"

"I care not what others so wholly unconnected to me might think."

"Then perhaps for once, you might look beyond your self-centred naïveté and consider the reputation of Pemberley!"

"How dare you?"

"How dare *you*—is the better question? This is one instance in which you will not have your way."

A standoff ensued. After a lengthy exchange, they reached a compromise of sorts. Elizabeth agreed to Darcy's request to accompany her to Lambton in his carriage. A mutually advantageous situation—not that either of the two was about to own it.

Once in Lambton, the earlier tension of the morning faded amidst the refreshing diversion of strolling about at leisure and browsing the local bookstore, providing Darcy with the opportunity to purchase several books, including some that Elizabeth wanted. They walked along the streets, arm in arm. Elizabeth delighted in exposing Darcy to many locally enjoyed pastimes. She even introduced him to the joyous admiration of window displays, for never had he even considered such an endeavour.

After they had enjoyed a satisfying meal at the Rose and Crown, another of Elizabeth's schemes and a first for the young Master of Pemberley, where she drank several glasses of wine to his one, it was time to return to Pemberley. Having imbibed enough wine to elevate her spirits without affecting her intellect, but rather her inhibitions, Elizabeth took hold of Darcy's arm upon his entering the carriage and did not relinquish it, even as they rode along. Their intimacy warmed Darcy's heart.

"I apologise for my attitude earlier in refusing to allow you to walk to Lambton. I had a most unpleasant experience with one of my tenants. I am afraid I may have taken it out on you," he said, his hand resting upon her hands on his arm, as he gazed out the window.

"There is enough blame for us both. I am your guest after all; I should honour your wishes."

"A most honoured guest, I assure you," he said as he turned to look upon her face.

"Thank you."

"These woods can be rather dangerous once outside the boundaries of Pemberley. I should never forgive myself if anything unfortunate befell you."

"Yes, you are forever my protector," she teased.

"Or so, I aspire to be. I care about you deeply."

"Deeply? And how would you say you express those deep sentiments? Do you regard me as you would a sister ... a friend ... or perhaps even a lover, Mr. Darcy?"

"A sister? I certainly do not," he said with conviction.

"A friend? Certainly, we are no doubt dear friends," he allowed.

"A lover? I have had lovers in the past. Now, I wish for something more," he confessed.

"What a shame," Elizabeth responded, "for I dearly wish for you to be *my* lover."

She is playing with fire. "Perhaps we both might be careful what we wish for."

Unabashed, she stated calmly, "Oh! I am quite determined. I have given this considerable thought. It is indeed my greatest wish that you should be my lover. In fact, I wish to see you in my apartment tonight."

Darcy thought with considerable awe upon her audacious statement. *I must be dreaming. I do not dare pinch myself for fear I might awaken. Elizabeth's chambers—tonight?*

He hesitated no longer. "As you wish."

* * *

What was she thinking? She could not deny the truth of the matter any longer. She was attracted to Darcy. She trusted him like no other. She longed for a night of passion—with him.

Nevertheless, did she truly know what she was about? Before she had realised what was happening, she had invited Darcy to her room.

Elizabeth's curiosity finally had won out. Was it one too many assemblies or private dinner parties where she was forced to sit with the other matrons in the room, pretending to understand what they meant when they spoke of the sexual proclivities of men and women and marital relations (the pleasant and the not so pleasant aspects). Heaven forbid when she found herself in the awkward position of giving advice to prospective brides.

Elizabeth had suffered enough. Enough of being vulnerable and defenceless against men who looked at her evocatively, spoke to her suggestively.

She trusted Darcy. A clandestine affair such as she had proposed would require the utmost discretion. It was only one night, and no one must ever know. No other person existed upon whose discretion she would have confidently depended. Who better than a man she had come to esteem to accompany her on her long-anticipated widow's rite of passage?

She prepared for bed with the utmost care, donning her silken robe and nightgown. Elizabeth sat in front of the mirror and watched as the flicker of the candles on the vanity danced with the beads in her robe. It had been a part of her wedding trousseau, yet she had never worn it. This would make up for the wedding night she never had.

Elizabeth picked up her brush and slowly stroked her long dark tresses. She was indeed as nervous as a new bride. Elizabeth had thrown caution to the wind in inviting Darcy to her room. Now she was unsure. Would he be able to discern that she was nowhere near as experienced as she should be? What would he think of her then?

A light tap at the door signalled her decisive moment.

Darcy entered the room to behold the breath-taking vision of the woman he loved, seductively attired and looking more beautiful than even he had imagined. Except for his dinner jacket, he remained fully dressed even down to his boots. Whilst he had agreed to her scheme to meet her in her apartment, he did not know what to expect. A man who had felt less might have immediately seized such a tempting prospect as she presented.

He was determined to follow her lead. To his surprise, Elizabeth possessed none of the confidence she had displayed earlier when she invited him there. After a quarter of an hour of idle chatter that served no purpose whatsoever in furthering the night's cause, Darcy realised a different tack was called for.

"Why did you invite me to your apartment, Elizabeth?" Darcy asked, still standing in the same spot as when he had first entered the room. Elizabeth had yet to relinquish her spot, as well.

"I think that is rather obvious," Elizabeth stated uneasily.

"Obviously not," He graced her with a look that, though innocent enough on the surface, bespoke smouldering passion underneath.

"I ... I want to spend this night with you ... to give myself to you," said she, thinking this was not what she had expected. Why was he making this difficult? "Why did you come?"

"Because I am in love with you, and I want to make love to you, all night."

"Then we are in agreement."

"Are we in agreement, Elizabeth? Are you in love with me?"

Elizabeth broke their gaze and lowered her eyes. She studied the pattern in the oriental rug as if in search of an answer. "I ... I like you. Our undeniable attraction is such that I no longer wish to ignore it." There, she had found her courage. She met his gaze once more.

"I want you to make love to me." That was it—the physical attraction, she considered, for she was convinced that she would never allow herself so intense an emotion as love.

"I prefer to wait until you more than just *like* me." He moved from his spot, but rather than approach her, he sat on the sofa, his long legs opened wide, and leaned forward, resting his elbows on his knees.

"I do not want to wait. I want you ... I need you. Why complicate matters with professions of love?"

"Do you know what you are suggesting?"

"Of course I do. Why do you insist upon treating me this way?"

"And what way is that, Elizabeth?"

"As if I do not know what I am about. I assure you, I do. I want you—I want you now."

The moment was impalpable. What to do—what to do? How many women had offered themselves to him? Yet, Elizabeth was not just any woman.

Darcy was torn. Taking the woman he loved up on her offer to give herself to him meant taking advantage of a naïve creature who thought she understood the ways of the world. Whatever he did, he surmised correctly it would hurt her if he rejected her. He did not want to reject her. His increasing desire of the moment was to make love to her, to make her feel like the woman she sought to be in inviting him to her bed.

Unhurriedly, he rose from his seat, walked to Elizabeth, and eased her silken robe from her shoulders, allowing it to drift to the floor. Standing behind her, he caressed her bare shoulders and leaned down to kiss the back of her neck. The sweet taste of her skin—so amazingly soft and delicate. He sensed her anxiety, her nervous quivers.

It is as though she has never been kissed this way.

He silently persuaded her around to face him. Darcy brushed his thumb along her lips as he studied her face. He adored her. He pressed his soft, warm lips to her forehead, her eyebrows, her cheekbones, the corners of her mouth—seductively returning his deep, arresting eyes to her face with each kiss.

Eventually, tilting his head slightly, Darcy leaned forward and pressed his lips against hers. His eyes closed, he proceeded gently, slowly urging her lips apart.

His lips ... exquisite. Elizabeth could never have imagined such intoxicating pleasure from a kiss. His lips were the first to have ever touched hers.

Her artless responses to his touch gave him pause.

"You are a vision," he whispered softly. Taking her hand, he led her to the sofa, whereupon he sat next to her and gathered her into his arms. With Elizabeth in his comforting embrace, her head resting on his chest, he coaxed her to place her feet upon the cushion and simply relax—promising her that they had the entire night to allow their love-making to unfold. First, his greatest desire was that they sit together and become comfortable with each other, with her cuddled in his arms next to him.

Darcy traced his fingers along Elizabeth's earlobes, her neckline, as he massaged her hand resting upon her lap, fondled her fingers and excited her senses with whispers of enticingly suggestive thoughts in her ear—the warmth of his voice inviting her to let go of any inhibitions.

As the hour passed, Darcy and Elizabeth remained seated on the sofa as he touched and caressed her everywhere in easy reach of his hands until she relaxed in his arms. Soon he pulled her onto his lap and commenced kissing her, suckling her and stroking her in all the spots predestined to deepen her pleasure. He lifted her into his arms and took her to her bed. Before she calmed, he joined her, and employed his extraordinarily precise lips to give her pleasure once more.

As wonderfully euphoric as Elizabeth was, sensations of longing filled her deep inside. Her body screamed for answers to the aching questions that always arose when the two of them were alone. Answers only he could provide. Moreover, he had yet to take his own pleasure.

"What about you? Will you not ... continue?" she whispered as she rested in his embrace—having come this far, it was her greatest desire they complete their daring dance of discovery.

He placed a silencing finger gently to her lips, followed by a light brush of his own. "Not tonight. I am content to hold you. Lie here and rest."

"Will you stay with me? Please do not leave me," she said as she clung to him tightly.

"I am afraid I cannot spend the entire night with you, but I promise I will stay as long as it takes until you fall deeply asleep," he whispered. He bestowed a tender kiss to her lips.

Elizabeth woke the next morning with the same thoughts that filled her mind when she had fallen asleep in Darcy's arms. Certainly one might experience consummation without passion—but such passion without consummation. Yet, it was the most magnificent experience of her life. She was sure she desired him more than ever now that she had a taste of fulfilment.

"But he said he was in love with me. No, no. It is not love. It cannot be love. Infatuation perhaps—combined with a deep, abiding friendship and powerful physical attraction," she voiced softly.

Sitting up in bed, Elizabeth noticed a note on her pillow.

Dearest Elizabeth,
Never have I experienced a more beautiful night. I can scarcely wait to see you this morning. Meet me in my private study.
Affectionately yours,
FD

Chapter 15 – So little endeavour at civility

"This is all the reply which I am to have the honour of expecting! I wish to hear why I am thus rejected, and with so little endeavour at civility."

Not that she was uncivil in any way. When Darcy had asked Elizabeth if she would do him the honour of accepting his proposal of marriage, after offering his whole heart in hand with words of love, affection, and deep esteem, she did not express any sort of appreciation of the honour he bestowed. She simply said no.

She had not been entirely caught off guard by his proposal. He said as much and demonstrated as well that he would not commit to her as anything other than his wife. Moments earlier, she had stood frozen outside the closed door of his study pondering his note.

What did I do? Was it unreasonable to have expected a single night of pleasure in his arms—that on the morning after, all would be the same as ever between the two of them? Had she encouraged his expectations that something more lasting would result from her impetuous act the evening before?

Elizabeth had walked into his study, determined that she could not accept, she would not accept an offer of marriage. She believed it beyond her power to accept him, convinced she could never make him happy, that the passion they shared for each other would fade and that his subsequent loss of interest in her would involve them both in misery of the acutest kind. Still, she owed him more than a heartless rejection. This man whom she had come to trust and esteem deserved better than that.

"I shall never marry again." She saw the hurt in his eyes. "I do care for you." She turned away from him in an effort not to witness the pain she was inflicting. "You are still a young man. You would be much better off with a younger woman, an innocent, who will be yours and yours alone. You deserve more than a woman who has given herself to another. I had my chance for happiness. I shall not take away yours."

Darcy spoke not a word. Elizabeth found his silence dreadful, the roar of the clock on the mantel deafening.

"While I have not had the honour of meeting the young lady myself, I have heard of Miss de Bourgh and your presumed attachment to her. She is sure to make a proper wife."

Darcy took a moment to consider how she had drawn that conclusion. *Wickham!* Deciding to centre his attentions on the matter at hand, he said, "Surely you do not expect me to walk away as if nothing is between us. Not after last night. Everything is changed."

"I grant you what we shared was beautiful, but it is not as though either of us has never enjoyed such passions before." Though words utterly lacking in sincerity, what else might she say without admitting the improbable truth?

"I can honestly say that I have not," he said. "I have never been so much in love before, and in my life, I have never made love to anyone as I made love to you."

Their eyes met as she turned to face him. She refused to consider the intensity of his affirmations of love. "But you did not—you did not give yourself completely."

"Elizabeth, what I did was done only for you. Be honest with yourself. You have never experienced such passion before last night. I want to share such pleasures with you every night for the rest of our lives."

He approached her and took her by the hand. "I did not make love to you completely because you deserve much better than to give yourself to me outside of marriage."

"What about what I want?" she asked, withdrawing her hand as she took a few steps back.

"I truly believe you are too naïve to discern what you want, Elizabeth. You have lived under the pretence of being experienced and worldly for so long, and rather than face what you know in your heart and soul as the truth, you willingly throw away your chances of happiness with both hands."

"You are mistaken. You know nothing about me," she protested.

"What more do I need to know, Elizabeth ... other than I love you with all my heart?"

"If one is to marry at all, then it is better done based upon one's head, rather than one's heart." As if to combat the incredulous turn of his countenance, she improved her tone in an attempt to render a persuasive argument.

"Think about it. A marriage between us defies reason. You, a younger man with your whole life before you, would suffer all the disadvantages in such an unequal alliance, whereas I would reap all the advantages. I am older. I am widowed. I offer no fortune, no connections. You risk the censure of your family, your friends, and society in general."

He started but said nothing. She continued, "No, I will not bear responsibility for exposing you to the world for its derision. I am convinced you must marry someone of your own sphere, someone younger and maidenly, or better still—honour your duty to your family and marry your cousin Anne de Bourgh."

"I am my own master. I shall marry where I choose. I choose you." He approached her and took her into his arms. He kissed her on her temple. "Do you no longer think of yourself as young? You are young and beautiful. I love you, Elizabeth. I ask you to be my wife. To share my life, my home, my bed ... please, say you will."

"I shall never marry again. I have offered myself to you, and I would do so again. However, I will not marry you."

"You offer yourself to me as what, my mistress?" He released her from his embrace and stepped away.

"No—not that. Never that. I shall not subordinate myself to any man," she declared, the thoughts in her mind returning to talk in town of the life of a mistress as certainly nothing worth coveting; an unwed woman as much the property of the man as a wife to her husband, as far as Elizabeth was concerned.

Taken aback, Darcy uttered, "So, you have it in mind to share my bed when it suits you, and then what, return to Bingley's home at your leisure?"

It would have been pointless to argue that she had only desired a single night of passion—not after the last night. "And why not? My brother and sister have opened their home to me. My brother's home is now my home, for as long as I wish."

"Elizabeth, you are not thinking this through. There are consequences to what you are suggesting—devastating consequences, not just for you but your family. Any child we might conceive would be considered a bastard, his birth greeted with derision rather than joy. I shall not be a party to it. I am in love with you. I have been since I first laid eyes on you," Darcy declared. "But I will not consent to become your lover without a commitment of marriage," he painfully and resolutely affirmed.

"I do not believe in love at first sight. Love at first sight is akin to nothing more than infatuation. Infatuation does not last. Once it is gone, then where would we be? I find it is wiser to indulge our passions while they last, and then be free to go in separate paths once they fade —as they most certainly will!"

"Think of it as infatuation if that is what gets you through the day, Elizabeth," he said, as he reclaimed her in his arms and kissed her so passionately her knees buckled. "But when you are alone in bed each night, recalling the pleasure of my touch, how it feels when I hold you, how I want to make you feel over and over as my wife, know that what I have for you is undying love."

Darcy started kissing her again, sweet, tender kisses along her face, her neckline. He picked her up and carried her to his chair, where they soon lost themselves in an amorous abyss.

Her responses to his kisses, his caresses, strengthened his ardour. Neither of the two wanted the moment to end. Darcy, if not Elizabeth, realised that it must end. A future between the two of them outside of wedlock was not even a possibility he was willing to consider.

How can she respond as she does with me now and not agree to marry me? We belong together, yet she will not admit it. That she aspires to separate our physical attraction from an emotional attachment is inconceivable, when we might have it all.

How could she have ever loved and been loved before and not know that I adore her? Ceasing his kisses, he tried reasoning with her once more.

After brushing dishevelled strands of hair from her face, he traced his thumb against her cheekbone. "I know you care for me as much as I care for you. You are making excuses—nonsensical excuses at that. You are far too headstrong and wilful for the opinion of others to persuade you against your purposes.

"What is the true reason for your reluctance? Why do you refuse? Is it because of your late husband—your love for him? Do you believe you will dishonour your first marriage should you choose to marry again so soon?"

In a staggering outburst, she escaped his affectionate embrace and cried out, "You cannot be more mistaken! I did not choose that marriage! I was forced into it! I never loved him! I do not believe in love, and I certainly do not believe in marriage!" The intensity of her confession prompted Elizabeth to back further away.

Darcy did not believe his ears. How was it possible that what she had just said was true? *Forced into marriage to a man she did not love.* He recalled Caroline Bingley's words, "One might as well have called it a love match because she made no secret of her regard for him." However, Elizabeth's own assertion that she never loved her late husband must be held as truth. *Why has she allowed so many, including me, to believe otherwise and for so long?*

Darcy stared at Elizabeth in stunned silence with an expression of mingled incredulity and disillusionment. The pause was to Elizabeth's sentiments abysmal. That he should learn the truth in that way, was nothing she would have envisioned.

The ensuing silence seemingly lasted forever, but in reality, less than a minute had passed before a knock at the door interrupted their heart-wrenching standoff. After allowing a few moments to pass, during which Elizabeth checked her appearance, Darcy answered the door. A footman handed him an urgent express for the Bingleys. Elizabeth seized the opportunity to take the letter to her brother herself.

"We shall finish this discussion after breakfast, Elizabeth."

"No, Mr. Darcy ... we will not."

"Do not do this," he pleaded one last time.

"I have given you my final answer, and I shall not change my mind. I will not marry you. Please excuse me, sir." She left the room without daring to look back at him to witness the pain she had inflicted on one so dear to her.

Chapter 16 – Such terms of cordiality

"Darcy, I must beg your discretion in the matter I am about to disclose. My dear Jane received a letter from her sister Mary, in which she informs us that Lydia has run away. She has thrown herself into the power of George Wickham," Bingley despaired, wringing his hands as he paced the floor. After listening attentively to Bingley's account of what had happened in Brighton—the reckless young girl had left the protection of her guardians to elope with the officer, but all the evidence had suggested they never made it farther than London— Darcy spoke at last.

"My God! What has been done, what has been attempted to recover her?" He was stunned. He fought the urge to race to Elizabeth's side. *She must be devastated.*

"Mr. Bennet has gone to London to meet Mr. Gardiner and determine what must be done. However, I fear nothing can be done. How does one work on such a man? How does one go about discovering them?"

"This is grave indeed."

"Indeed, I believe I must set out for London at once, to aid in the search, but Jane is needed back in Hertfordshire to attend her mother during this taxing time."

"Of course, you must escort Mrs. Bingley and Mrs. Calbry to Hertfordshire immediately. I will go to London and undertake my own search. Given the delicate nature of all this, I shall not impose upon Mr. Gardiner or Mr. Bennet, but rather I will deal directly with you." Darcy stood from his chair and walked over to his liquor cabinet. He needed a drink.

What has that scoundrel done? Why has he preyed on the Bennet family? The heat of the amber liquid as it slid down his throat tempered his rage. Darcy filled a second glass and handed it to his friend. "I want no one to learn of my involvement, you understand. Meet me at my London townhouse the moment you arrive from Hertfordshire."

Amidst Bingley's fervent protests that it was his family and his duty to take on the unpleasant business, Darcy explained that he understood Wickham's character, his habits. He could provide invaluable assistance. He assured Bingley that he would stand by him, no matter the outcome, but he would do all he might in bringing about a more favourable one than was thought possible by the family.

As he had never actually met Mr. Bennet nor Mr. Gardiner, he did not want to impose upon them in Cheapside during such a difficult time for the family. Despite his friendship with Bingley, he could claim nothing more than a casual acquaintance with the Bennet family proper. He was determined to stay in the background.

"Do not worry, my friend. I will do all in my power to make certain that this matter is resolved, but time is of the essence if we are to protect the reputation of the family."

While Bingley set off to inform Jane and Elizabeth of their immediate departure, Darcy remained behind to arrange for his own sojourn to town.

Darcy accompanied his departing guests to their awaiting carriage. Though neither Bingley nor Jane suspected anything untoward between Darcy and Elizabeth, other than that they shared an unusually strong friendship, they inferred enough to allow them some moments of privacy to say good-bye.

Darcy and Elizabeth silently regarded the countenance of the other as if to commit to memory every aspect—both recognising how unlikely it was that they should ever meet each other again. Even if, because of their common connection with Bingley, they did see each other, never again would it be on such terms of cordiality as had marked their past few months in each other's company. They had reached an impasse. He loved her. He had hoped to spend the rest of his life with her. She did not believe in love and would never commit to the uncertain fate of marriage again.

Darcy broke the silence as he took her hand and placed a note within. "I ask that you do me the honour of reading this letter." His voice held none of the command of the haughty gentleman of her earliest acquaintance. He sounded like a dispirited, broken-hearted lover.

"Farewell, Mr. Darcy." Her silent acceptance of the letter signalled her intention to read it.

"Farewell, Mrs. Calbry," he said as he handed her into the carriage. He watched the carriage pull away.

Farewell, Elizabeth.

* * *

With the carriage pulling away from Pemberley House, Elizabeth turned back and saw Darcy still standing there ... seeing and sensing the pain she had inflicted upon him by her rejection.

I know in my heart that he is much better off without me than not, thought she with a sudden, sharp feeling akin to regret. *In time, he will know it too. Now, with this latest scandal, yes, he is far better off without me.*

To be mistress of all this might have been something, she silently reflected, catching sight of what had become one of her favourite paths.

The farther their carriage drew away from Pemberley, the less certain she became of her ability to maintain her resolve. Was he better off without her—was she better off without him? No doubt, if she were ever inclined to marry again ... if not for the dreadful experience of her first marriage, Mr. Darcy would be the only man for her. However, each semblance of regret was quickly quailed by the harsh truth—her marriage had been horrific; she would never chance such a fate again. Further conjecture on the matter of matrimony was pointless.

Moreover, as she threw a retrospective glance over the whole of their acquaintance, so full of contradictions and varieties, she sighed at the satirical thought that those feelings that should have promoted its continuance had instead brought about a parting of their ways.

After many hours had passed, Jane and Bingley gave in to the sweltering demand of the hot midsummer day and the steady sound of the carriage rolling down the road. The two having fallen asleep, Elizabeth was finally at leisure to read Darcy's letter.

Dear Mrs. Calbry,

Be not alarmed, Madam, on receiving this letter. I shall not repeat the sentiments of this morning. Rather, I write to express my sorrow for your distress over this most unfortunate circumstance of your sister, Miss Lydia. Fear not, I honour Bingley as my closest friend; I shall not repeat a word of what he has told me. I pray for a happier conclusion than is yet anticipated.

This shall all pass with time. As it does, I wish to express my sincere hope that you one day will allow happiness back into your life. I had long watched you at times when you believed yourself to be unobserved. I saw a woman pretending to be that which you are not—pretending nothing was missing in your life.

Your innate charm, your wit, and your vitality insist that, for the greatest part of your life, you had to have known that something of which I write. As much as I care for you, I thought I might be the one to help you reclaim those feelings once again. I realise now that is not a possibility. One chooses happiness.

I fear you will never allow yourself any happiness until you first let go of the hurt and anger of your past by allowing yourself to grieve the loss of your youth, your innocence, and even the loss of your late husband. Allow yourself to grieve the loss of your youth and innocence after having been forced into a marriage that you did not want. Grieve the loss of your husband, whom you may not have loved, but whom you vowed to honour and obey. Let go of all the pain and the guilt associated with that time of your life, and open yourself to begin anew.

I hope and trust that you will heed these words, in time, allowing yourself to be worthy of happiness again, and that you will experience the love you so richly deserve.

I will only add, God bless you,
Fitzwilliam Darcy

Chapter 17 – Of soon knowing by heart

Confined to her bed, prostrate with grief, Mrs. Bennet, to whose apartment they all repaired upon their arrival at Longbourn, received them just as might be expected. Tears, lamentations of regret, invectives against the villainous conduct of Wickham, and complaints of her own sufferings and ill-usage poured from her room, down the stairs, and throughout the manor making it impossible that any of the inhabitants of Longbourn would be unaware of her sufferings.

Nothing they did consoled her. She taxed everyone who would be taxed including Elizabeth—who, though reluctant to return to Longbourn, was compelled to do so for Jane's sake, even if for the sake of no one else. Her father's decision to remain in town in search of Lydia made the situation tolerable for Elizabeth to return to her childhood home after so many months of self-imposed exile. Elizabeth appreciated being of use. The care of her mother provided a much-needed distraction for her and allowed her to think of anything but what troubled her most.

Reflection was reserved for solitary hours, but whenever she found herself to be alone, she gave way to it as the greatest relief; and not a day went by without a solitary walk, during which she indulged in all the discontent of unpleasant recollections. Mr. Darcy's letter, she now knew by heart. She had studied every sentence, every word. Each time, her sentiments towards its author differed widely. The poignancy of his words haunted her.

Let go of the guilt and the pain.

Guilt? Elizabeth accounted for nothing she had done that should cause her to suffer guilt of any kind. *Daniel's actions and his actions alone had led to the forced marriage.* Sure, he had been her favourite, and all of Meryton had known it. Had she not been so openly fond of him, would the scandal have been lessened? Might the compromising circumstances have been more easily explained away? Would her father have listened to her, stood up for her in the midst of a scandal that threatened her entire family's reputation, and not forced her to accept the marriage?

Guilt? Yes, she prayed every day to be freed from Daniel, to be released from that farce of a marriage. When informed of his fatal carriage accident, she had silently rejoiced. Her prayers had been answered; it had been a dream come true. However, she did play the part of a grieving widow for a full year and a day, convincing everyone of her despair. All this while her sister Jane and her new husband put their own lives on hold, as she counted the days until she could return to her former self.

Pain? Did she know pain? Was anything more painful than the loss of esteem for one's parent? What was more painful than being forced from the comforts of her childhood home? Forced to live with people who held her in contempt, looked down upon her, and treated her more as a guest who had overstayed her welcome than a member of the family. How painful! Forced to marry a man who showed no proper consideration for her, who exposed her to his infidelity night after night.

What had Mr. Darcy meant to accomplish by writing such a letter —one that would force those long-repressed memories to come flooding back? Such was Elizabeth's familiar refrain.

Alas, those painful memories came rushing back with a vengeance, drowning her sensibilities in grief and despair. Elizabeth had suffered alone for a long time. The unhappy defects of her family had often proved a subject of heavy chagrin. Even before her wretched marriage to Daniel Calbry, the idea of matrimony had held little appeal. She thought little of her parents' marriage, save its satirical nature. A poor example indeed, for her father did not treat her mother with esteem. Elizabeth had found this unacceptable, but as the favourite child of her father, had been disinclined to judge him harshly.

Yet, her father had always been contented with laughing at her mother and her sisters, and would never exert himself to restrain the wild giddiness of his youngest daughters. With Lydia's elopement and Elizabeth's long disillusionment with him during the time she felt she had needed him most, she perceived his neglect of his family in a far more unforgiving light than perhaps he deserved.

At least he had travelled to London in search of Lydia; what was more honourable than that? Elizabeth was near conceding that point until she learnt that it was through Bingley's efforts that Lydia had been recovered and Wickham forced to marry her. Her brother had remained in London to carry the scheme through. Her father had chosen to return to the comforts of Longbourn and the solitude of his library, rather than remain in London, leaving Bingley in his stead to perform the unpleasant duties that should have been his.

Mr. Bennet's return bearing news of Lydia's pending nuptials saw the miraculous recovery of Mrs. Bennet to her former spirits. She pronounced that all the servants should have a glass of punch while she set forth to spread the joyful news to all her Meryton neighbours that would hear it. Mrs. Bennet was all a flutter with the excitement of planning the wedding and wedding breakfast when Mr. Bennet abruptly ended her raptures with the pronouncement that Lydia had behaved abominably, her actions nearly ruining the reputation of the entire family, and it certainly would have been so, had it not been for the providential actions of his son-in-law. Finally, he stated his intentions never to receive his daughter and her future husband at Longbourn again.

Mr. Bennet's return meant Jane and Elizabeth were no longer needed to attend their *ailing* mother. Elizabeth, now spared the task of returning to Longbourn, had never encountered her father in his home even once. She had departed Longbourn with a greater feeling of indignation and lack of esteem for her father than ever before.

The coming days, long and melancholy, brought much of the same unpleasant recollection to Elizabeth's mind. The nasty weather added to the gloom. Exasperated, Elizabeth had always fancied herself not formed for ill humour. Her philosophy had long been to "think only of the past as its remembrance gives you pleasure." Alas, such was not the case.

It was impossible to consider any aspect of her past, present or future with pleasure without recalling the pained look on Mr. Darcy's face when he last spoke to her, or without reciting in her mind every word of his letter. If she could but see him again, she would make him understand it was not her fault and certainly not her choice that she was opposed to marriage. She had been wronged, entirely through the acts of others.

What is the point? He decreed that I am unhappy and then turned his back on me.

More and more Elizabeth began to choose the solitude of her room over the company of her family. The advent of guests garnered a lacklustre reception from Elizabeth. Acquaintances likened her lethargy to one who was in mourning and often wondered what had brought on such a gloomy state.

Jane wished to bear it no longer. Since their departure from Pemberley, she had witnessed a steady decline in her sister's spirits. At first, she attributed it to Lydia's elopement, but that misfortunate occurrence had resulted in a satisfactory conclusion for all concerned. Jane wondered what else might be the cause of Elizabeth's malaise.

Jane knew more than anyone how Elizabeth kept everything of her private life to herself. It would not do. She was determined to reach out to her sister—to get her to open up. Jane knocked at her sister's closed door. Elizabeth had not come down for breakfast that day. It was already past noon. Her maid responded to Jane's inquiry into her sister's health with the news that she had not ventured beyond her room, not even for an early morning walk. Jane grew more worried with each second that passed with no answer until, some minutes later, after repeated knocks, she entered on her on accord in response to the turn of the door key from inside the room.

Elizabeth had awakened long before dawn, after a fitful night, with an epiphany. Darcy's words advising her to be honest with herself, mingled with his words in his letter urging her to let go of her pain and anger, had chased her in her dreams, and allowed no escape until finally she woke. Unable to return to sleep, she had no choice but to suffer dispassionate reflection on her past, to allow for her own role in her dreadful experience. Foremost in her thinking was an acknowledgement of the duty of accepting responsibility as an adult, accepting her role in choosing to respond to adversity as she had. Although one cannot control what happens to them, one can control how they respond. Her choice had been a hopeless one. *I chose to hold others entirely at*

fault—to consider myself blameless. This realisation did not come easily for Elizabeth. It required a different way of thinking than that to
which she had been accustomed: who she had been, who she was, and
who she would be.

"Lizzy, what on earth is the matter?" Jane asked as she rushed to
her sister perched on her bed, her knees clutched closely to her chest.
Jane looked into her sister's eyes. "You have been crying! What has
happened to upset you?"

"Oh Jane, I have been such a fool," Elizabeth started, "it is finally
dawning on me how selfish I have been—how unthinking I have been
towards everyone. For months, I have courted self-pity, thinking only
of myself, what I want, what I feel. I have given little thought to how
my actions might have affected those around me."

"No, Lizzy, you are being too harsh on yourself. We all know
how much you have suffered these past months with the loss of your
husband—the abandonment of his family."

"But that is just it. The fact is, Jane, I have been dishonest in allowing everyone to think that my marriage was a happy one."

"Whatever do you mean?"

"Jane, it was the most wretched experience of my life," she
began.

Elizabeth confided everything to Jane relating to her horrible
marriage to Daniel, starting with what she had witnessed in the copse
between him and the servant girl, how it led to the compromising
situation necessitating the forced marriage, and ending with her poor
treatment at the hands of his relatives upon his death.

"Why did you not tell me of your suffering? I might have been of
service to you. I, more than anyone, know how you tend to keep things
to yourself ... to suffer in silence; however, had I even suspected, had I
not been so caught up in my own wedded bliss, I might have been
more of a sister and confidante to you."

"You have always been of great comfort to me, and I am grateful
you took me into your home when I felt everything was lost, but this
was something I needed to sort through myself; which I might not have
even now, if not for Mr. Darcy."

"Mr. Darcy? What has he to do with any of this?"

"Everything, I assure you," Elizabeth stated. "Suffice it to say that
we have grown close in a short time. You cannot have missed it. He

gave me a parting letter when we abruptly left Pemberley, in which he encouraged me to let go of the pain and anger I have been burying for so long." Elizabeth's response to Jane, though honest, was not as forthcoming as it might have been. Jane had no way of knowing that, however.

She continued to offer her solace. "You are correct, Lizzy. I had not failed to notice that the two of you had grown close towards the end of the Season, not that I think it is a bad thing, mind you ... far from it. I have always held Mr. Darcy in esteem."

"I am ashamed to admit how abominably I have behaved towards him. As you well know, I judged him severely at the start of our acquaintance, but once I realised that he meant no harm—that he was only looking out for my best interests—" she proceeded once more.

Elizabeth began to recount the story of what had happened in town; everything—how Mr. Darcy had berated her repeatedly on her unguarded behaviour, the wager, the unfortunate encounter with Lord Winthrop, and Lady Hargrove's duplicity. The drawn-out, emotional exchange found Elizabeth doing most of the talking—Jane, the listening. At the end of it, Jane was shocked and her countenance betrayed her abhorrence! Poor Jane! To learn that such wickedness existed in the world. In a rare display, she enthusiastically expressed her utter antipathy without once attempting to find any decency in either of the two scoundrels who had presented themselves as friends.

"It feels good being forthcoming about all this," Elizabeth confessed, fully aware she had so much yet to tell, but satisfied to avoid any such heartfelt revelations until she better understood it all herself. "Thank you, dearest Jane, for listening to me so patiently."

"Fear not, I shall always be here for you, and I shall not allow you to keep things to yourself ever again," Jane promised. "I shall be as persistent in forcing your confidences as Mama has been in finding husbands for us all!"

Chapter 18 – Disguise of every sort

B ingley stood in Darcy's foyer, hat in hand, about to set off for Hertfordshire.

"Darcy, I appreciate all you did in recovering Lydia and in bringing about the marriage to Wickham. Will you not reconsider and accept my invitation to Netherfield Park?"

"I fear I must decline. The inducement of spending another minute in the company of the *newly-weds*," Darcy spat the term, "is reason enough for me to decline. However, it is more than that. I am expected in Kent. I will spend a few weeks there before returning to Derbyshire with Georgiana."

"Capital! By the time you depart Kent, the Wickhams will have headed north. Georgiana is welcome to join us." Bingley believed that if no one else, than certainly Jane must be made aware of the truth behind the Bennet family's salvation. He wanted to afford Jane the opportunity to thank him in person. Darcy suspected as much.

"Bingley, need I remind you that no one must know of my part in the recovery of your sister." Darcy scoffed at the irony of his predicament. He, after all, trusted a known scoundrel and his flighty bride to keep their mouths closed.

"That being said, I shall not fault you, should you decide to take your wife into your confidence. I leave it to you to decide. I require no one's gratitude."

Darcy waved his friend off with a conviction there was little chance he would return to Netherfield Park, not then, perhaps not ever, though he did not say as much to Bingley.

The truth of the matter was that it was unendurable that Darcy should return to Pemberley with the memories of the time spent with Elizabeth so fresh in his mind. He was always content to spend time with his family, and the fact that Georgiana had grown close to not only Anne, but Mrs. Collins as well, was deemed as sufficient grounds not to separate her from her friends.

Whenever Darcy would give himself leave for uninhibited thoughts, those thoughts tended toward Elizabeth. What each of the two wanted opposed the wishes of the other. Darcy needed to learn indifference—what better place than Kent to begin.

Time with my family will serve me well.

Elizabeth's rejection of his offer of marriage had hurt Darcy even worse than he bothered to admit. Always accustomed to getting his way, he had not yet learnt to consider her rejection without some acrimony of spirit. Acrimony and disappointment. His recovery of her sister at considerable discomfort and expense to himself evidenced his willingness to do anything for her. Though disguise of every sort was his abhorrence, it had to be that way, for he had not done it to seek her gratitude, but rather to encourage her felicity. In spite of the fact that he believed himself to be in love with her, he would not suffer his pride or his views in attempting to change the mind of one whose wishes so decidedly opposed his own.

Nevertheless, feelings such as those did not prevent his missing her—he longed for her, though he endeavoured not to by focusing his attentions upon Georgiana and Anne.

Any time not spent with the two of them was spent in solitude. Solitary moments afforded reflection of the dichotomy of events of the past months—sometimes with joy, oftentimes with pain, always with solemn regret.

* * *

Mr. and Mrs. Wickham accompanied Bingley upon his return to Netherfield Park. Mr. Bennet stuck to his resolve never to receive the thoughtless couple at Longbourn, despite Mrs. Bennet's fierce protest to the contrary. Charles and Jane reluctantly opened their home to the couple during their brief stay in Hertfordshire, before the newly minted Mr. and Mrs. Wickham were to venture on to Newcastle.

The entire week, little of anything else was possible beyond attending the newly-weds. Lydia had the gall to request the honour of a ball in a celebration of her nuptials, prompting poor Bingley to laugh aloud at her audacity. The Bingleys held a wedding breakfast for the Wickhams instead that comprised a guest list of only the immediate family and the Phillipses. Mr. Bennet did not deign to recognise the travesty of a marriage with his attendance.

Later that night, while Jane, Elizabeth, and Lydia sat in the drawing room awaiting the company of Bingley and Wickham, Lydia thought it a fitting occasion to entertain her sisters with tales of her recent amorous interludes with her dear husband. Jane and Elizabeth listened to their boisterous younger sister's accounts with an odd mixture of curiosity and disgust.

Alas, Lydia's candid long-windedness proved too much for either of the older women's sensibilities. Elizabeth was unable to refrain from interruption.

"Perhaps in such cases as this, what goes on in the bedchamber should stay in the bedchamber!"

"La!" the younger woman shrieked, "I should not be surprised to hear those words coming from you!"

Elizabeth, caught off guard by her sister's line of attack, wondered what she could mean. *No one knows of my secret.*

She had spoken to Jane of most of the misfortunes of her marriage, but with one glaring omission. Some matters she kept to herself. As regarded the specific horrors of her marriage, she kept her silence, thinking Jane would never comprehend such evil. Why trouble her with the sordid details? She had suffered her hardships and risen above them; there was no need in introducing Jane to the realities of such humiliations.

Lydia put an end to Elizabeth's silent reverie. "It is no secret my dear Wickham was your favourite! You are jealous I have stolen him from you."

Shock and relief blanketed her countenance. "You are more than welcome to him. As much as it pains me to say it, the two of you deserve each other!" Elizabeth shouted in frustration, perhaps not truly intending her youngest sister should be reconciled to such a state. She was unable to retract her statement, for Lydia did not keep silent for long.

"Thank you very much, Lizzy, for allowing that I am welcome to my own husband," Lydia retorted and picked up right where she left off before her sister's boorish interruption.

The arrival of Wickham ended Lydia's ramblings, prompting Elizabeth, and no doubt Jane too, if she would but own it, to rejoice in silence. Never had they been so glad to greet Mr. Wickham!

* * *

The storm clouds that had lingered over Hertfordshire for the past days cleared, giving rise to the warmth and pleasure of the sun. Elizabeth found it hard to remain indoors. Only the presence of George Wickham served as a source of vexation for her ever-reviving spirits. The week dragged on seemingly forever. Everywhere Elizabeth turned, she came across her new brother. One bright, sunny day, she strolled along, her mind deep in thought, when someone's approach aroused her notice.

Mr. Wickham! Before she could strike into another path, he overtook her.

"I pray I am not interrupting your solitary ramble, my dear sister?" said he, as he joined her.

"You certainly do," she replied with a smile, "but you are welcome to accompany me, of course."

I can do this. I only need to smile and nod in the appropriate places.

"I am delighted to hear that. We have always been good friends. Now we are better."

Elizabeth looked over her shoulder. *Where is Lydia when one requires her presence?* "Does anyone else plan to join us?"

"I do not know. Mrs. Bennet and Lydia are going in the carriage to Meryton. By the by, my wife tells me that you have actually seen Pemberley."

Smile.

"I almost envy you the pleasure. If not for the fact that it would be too much for me, I would take it in on my way to Newcastle."

Newcastle? Better, it was New Zealand. Where is New Zealand? Elizabeth pondered. *I shall make it my business to find out upon my return to the manor.*

After a brief period of awkward silence, he continued, "I was surprised to encounter Darcy in town last week. Our paths crossed quite a few times. I wonder what business he had there."

Mr. Darcy is in town! I thought he was in Derbyshire. "Perhaps preparing for his marriage with Miss de Bourgh," said Elizabeth pointedly. "It must be something particular, to take him to town during this time of year."

"Indeed. And Miss Darcy, have you had the chance to meet her?"

"Yes, I was introduced to her in town. I like her."

"I have heard, indeed, that she is uncommonly improved within this year or two. When I last saw her, she was not very promising. I am glad you liked her. I hope she will turn out well."

"I dare say she will. She has got over the most trying age."

"Did you go by the village of Kympton?"

Why would I go to Kympton? "I do not recollect that we did."

"I mention it, because it is the living which I ought to have had. What a delightful place it is! The Parsonage House is excellent. It would have suited me in every respect."

Goodness! He is self-centred. How did I not see him for the man he is before?

She had suffered enough of the conversation. She sought to end it quickly. Elizabeth relayed her understanding of the conditional bequeath, subject to the will of the present patron.

"Yes, but I told you so from the first, do you not remember?"

I hardly remember YOUR account, sir. "My memory serves me well; there was a time when sermon-making was not as agreeable to you as you profess at present. Pursuant to your determination of never taking orders, the business was completed accordingly."

"Indeed, dear sister, your account is not wholly without foundation. You may remember what I told you on that point, when first we talked of it."

Please, do not remind me, Mr. Wickham. They were now at the door. *I thought this walk might never end. I do not believe I have ever walked so fast.* "Come, Mr. Wickham, we are brother and sister, you know. Do not let us quarrel about the past. In the future, I hope we shall be always of one mind." She held out her hand as a measure of silent truce, and he bestowed the most awkward of kisses.

Mr. Wickham was satisfied with the conversation, and he never again distressed himself or provoked his dear sister Elizabeth by introducing the subject of it. She was pleased to find that she had said enough to keep him quiet.

Indeed, the day of the Wickhams' leave-taking could not come soon enough in Elizabeth's way of thinking. When at last the Wickhams departed Netherfield Park, an overwhelming sense of relief overcame all of its inhabitants, family and servants alike.

For Bingley, much of the distress over the secrecy of the whole Wickham debauchery lingered. Bingley grew wearier by the abundance of gratitude lavished upon him and found he could no longer bear the conspiracy of silence.

His anguish was painfully evident when, at last, he spoke to his wife. "I can bear this burden no longer, but Darcy swore me to secrecy."

"Whatever do you mean? Surely, Mr. Darcy did not intend that you should keep secrets from your wife," Jane interrupted. She looked up from the tangled mess of bright coloured ribbons in her lap, giving her husband her full attention.

"Well, actually he did just that," stated Bingley.

"If he knew how bothered you were by this great secret and how it was tearing at you, he would not want you to keep it locked inside," Jane coaxed her reluctant husband.

"I suppose you are correct. He did say he would not wholly object if I shared the confidence with you. I have said nothing because I did not want to put you in the position of keeping secrets from your sister. I must beg of your utmost discretion, my dear."

"What is it, Charles?" Jane asked with some growing sense of uneasiness. Her large blue eyes widened with worry.

"I have felt like such a cad since my return to Hertfordshire amidst the praises of our family for recovering Lydia."

"A cad, my dear? Why would you say such a thing? You deserve all our adoration and more. Where would we be during all this, had it not been for your gallantry?" she proudly asked her husband.

"But that is it. Darcy deserves all the credit. He did everything. He found them; he paid for Wickham's commission. Nothing was done, that he did not do himself. He would only allow me to discharge Wickham's debts here in Meryton, and he took care of the rest," Bingley confessed, grateful at last to have relinquished his borrowed feathers and given the praise where it was due.

"Such generosity!" Jane marvelled. Her angelic face hinted at confusion. "But why would he take it upon himself to do such a thing for a family so wholly unconnected to him as ours?" Jane wondered, suspecting whatever she might, but incredulous all the same.

"He said he felt responsible for Wickham's treachery because he did not expose him during his stay in Hertfordshire."

After spending some time talking it through, Jane was convinced they must express their gratitude to Mr. Darcy. In a manner reminiscent of her mother, she persuaded Charles to write to him, appealing, once more, for him to visit them at Netherfield Park upon his departure from Kent.

Chapter 19 – Every kind of pride

The footman handed an express to Charles. Excited to discover that it was from Darcy, he did not hesitate to read it in that instant. Jane was convinced Darcy's swift response was a sure indication of his intention of accepting the invitation. The change in her husband's countenance gave her pause.

"What does Mr. Darcy write to say? Does he accept our invitation to visit?"

Elizabeth felt a sudden fluttering in her stomach. *Mr. Darcy might visit Netherfield. Why has Jane kept it as a secret? Is it possible that I might see him again?*

"I am sorry, my dear. He writes to say that he is unable to accept. He has decided to remain in Kent, at least through the end of the summer. He speaks of his obligation to his family."

His obligation to his family, Elizabeth considered. *He remains in Kent since our departure from Pemberley. It has been well over a month. What exactly is his obligation to his family?* Unable to remain composed and with no desire to chance falling apart in front of her family, Elizabeth excused herself unceremoniously and raced upstairs to her apartment to mull over the implications.

Startled by her abrupt departure, Bingley looked towards Jane. "What on earth is the matter with Elizabeth? I hope she did not find anything disagreeable with the meal!" He picked up her plate of half eaten eggs in search of a clue in the mystery of his sister's behaviour.

"No—I am certain it is not that," Jane said as she proceeded to enlighten Charles. She concluded her speech by explaining that Mr. Darcy and Elizabeth had not parted on the best of terms.

"I fear I have been most insensitive." Bingley placed his linen napkin on his plate and arose from his chair. "I should apologise at once."

"No dear, allow me to handle this," Jane said as she stood to follow her sister.

* * *

His long fingers, first one, and then two, pushed deeper inside, a bit more, until he discovered the desired spot ... massaging in a come-hither fashion, gently at first, gradually increasing, firming the pressure. The tension building up inside, the warmth of his voice beckoning ... let go. Inviting.

Inviting! Darcy roused abruptly. Would he ever stop thinking of her? Longing for her? It was one thing to spend the night dreaming of her. He looked at the ornate mantle clock. *It is the middle of the morning.*

He knew he had no other choice than to decline the invitation to Netherfield Park and remain in Kent with his family. He owed it to himself, as well as his family, to remain in Kent a bit longer as he had promised.

More to the point, he dare not vouch for his ability to resist her with the temptation of spending night after night in her intimate company, their bedchambers silent footsteps apart. Perhaps in time, he would learn indifference. Until such time, he had no intention of going anywhere near Hertfordshire.

Meanwhile, Elizabeth having paced back and forth in her room, managed to envision many scenarios in a relatively short while. *All this time, he has not been at Pemberley with Georgiana as he had originally planned, but rather in Kent with his cousin, his presumed intended. Have I pushed him into another woman's arms? Could he love his cousin? Would he be happy with her after professing his undying love for me?*

During those fleeting moments in the breakfast room, as she had awaited with bated breath her brother's response to Jane's question of whether Mr. Darcy would be coming to Netherfield Park, Elizabeth's emotions had run the gamut from apprehension and dread, to exhilaration, and then to despair. She longed to hear her brother mention any word of him; she longed to see him again—even hoped that he might be invited to Netherfield Park and that he might agree to come.

Alas, he preferred to remain in Kent. *With his cousin, no doubt.* She was disheartened. *What would be his purpose, other than to offer for her?*

Elizabeth fretted. She had all but pushed him into Miss Anne de Bourgh's arms by her refusal. She imagined Mr. Darcy walking along, smiling adoringly at his cousin. The man she had fallen in love with. Her love for him—her regret of him, both now impossible to deny.

Jane came across Elizabeth in her room in a rather distressed and agitated state. She insisted that Elizabeth be forthright and tell her everything. Elizabeth sought to oblige.

Once Elizabeth confided in Jane about the marriage proposal at Pemberley, her rejection and his apparent resulting disdain, Jane, with a sense of relief, felt compelled to share what she knew of Darcy's involvement in the Wickham affair, now convinced of his motivations, because heretofore Bingley and she could not fathom his purpose. Mr. Darcy had done everything on behalf of Elizabeth.

Jane explained to Elizabeth that, by her husband's account, Mr. Darcy had ventured to town soon after they departed Pemberley, and had taken on himself the trouble and mortification attendant on such a search. Upon locating the nefarious gentleman, he had met, reasoned with, persuaded, and finally bribed Mr. Wickham to marry Lydia.

"So you see, he does not resent or disdain you. Why else would he do such a thing, if not for his deep admiration for you? What greater testament is there to the strength of his love? He would not allow the scandal to affect your chances of happiness even if such happiness is found with someone other than himself."

"Or perhaps something else prompted his actions," Elizabeth responded.

"What do you mean by that?"

"Perhaps it was his own guilt that compelled him to act," Elizabeth suggested as she discussed with Jane, everything that she knew of Wickham—everything that Darcy had confided in her; everything that he had not shared with Bingley. With a deep sense of remorse, Elizabeth stated, "Sometimes, I feel I might have prevented all that Lydia went through by being more open with my family."

"Do not fret. This was not your story to tell. But why should you or Mr. Darcy suffer the blame for Lydia's recklessness and our father's neglect?"

Elizabeth never suspected that Jane shared her same sensibility as it regarded their father's irresponsible treatment of their family. In perfect agreement that assignment of blame at that stage was pointless as Lydia appeared happy with the bed she had made, they decided to think no more on the matter.

"Lizzy, I feel awkward in having betrayed my husband's confidence, but you needed to know the truth."

"Fear not, I believe we are both guilty of breaking our promises of concealment to the men we love."

"Wait! Did you say love? Are you sincere, Lizzy? Do you love Mr. Darcy?"

"Indeed, I do. I imagine I must have loved him since our stay at Pemberley, but was unwilling or unable to see it." It felt right expressing her closely guarded sentiments aloud.

She loved him.

The two sisters embraced. "Lizzy, that is wonderful news indeed! The answer to my prayers was that you should meet and fall in love with a wonderful man, and you have."

"Dear Jane, I am afraid you will think badly of me once you learn the whole story of my acquaintance with Mr. Darcy."

"When have you ever known me to think badly of anyone?"

"Well, what about the time when—" Elizabeth began before Jane interrupted her.

"Oh hush, Lizzy, and tell me at once what you have managed to conceal for so long," Jane insisted.

Elizabeth described everything that occurred between Darcy and herself, even admitting she was the instigator. She confided that they had shared one night of intimacy, and yet she had refused his offer of marriage, truly believing she would never marry again. Elizabeth confessed to Jane that she had never known such passion until that night. Jane stared, coloured, gasped, and at times sat on the edge of her seat as she listened intently to Elizabeth's account.

"Well, tell me at once—what do you think? End my suspense. Have I finally managed to outdo myself in your eyes?"

Jane managed to keep her sister on tenterhooks as she contemplated her choice of words. Finally, she said, "Perhaps—it is only natural that you should wish to satisfy your curiosity—to know something of the passion you never experienced in your marriage. I shall not judge you. I applaud your bravery, dear sister."

Finally, Elizabeth confided to her sister the contents of Darcy's letter, sharing that he had asked her to open her heart to happiness. Elizabeth assured Jane that she had, that now she truly believed she would be happy again and even if it might be too late for a future with him, she would not give up on love.

Elizabeth was beginning to take comfort in having Jane as a confidante, in being open with someone she held so dear to her heart. Jane left Elizabeth in her apartment with the happy news of her own wedded bliss. Charles and she were expecting a child. Elizabeth received the news with delight for her sister and a measure of hope for herself.

* * *

The longer Darcy prolonged his visit, the greater the hope and comfort his aunt took that it should always be so. Darcy, her most beloved nephew, would forever remain nearby. She fancied that he might return to Pemberley at some point after the wedding, but it must not be for long. Very soon, she imagined that all her dreams, all her plans would come true. The two estates, at last, were to unite. The Darcys would make their home at Rosings Park. Rosings Park would be made as grand as Pemberley, she considered. No, Pemberley would be made as grand as Rosings Park!

The union, planned since the cousins' births, was to become a reality. How blessed would be that day.

Lady Catherine never confined her expectations to silent pondering. While one Darcy remained unaffected by a word she uttered, another Darcy was not at all oblivious. Georgiana was as thoroughly familiar with the tale of her brother's supposed destiny as one might have expected, having heard it repeated all her life and even more during her time at Kent over the past weeks. Pursuant to her brother's arrival, she could no longer remain unaffected.

How should she feel to have Anne as a sister? On the other hand, why was he even in Kent? Georgiana felt sure that her brother had fallen in love with Mrs. Elizabeth Calbry. Though she had yet to ascribe her own feelings on such an alliance, having learnt from her brother that she was invited to Pemberley for the summer was as sure a sign as any of an attachment.

Georgiana had grown exceedingly fond of her brother. He was the last man in the world who would intentionally give any woman the idea of his feeling for her more than he did. The marked attentions he showed towards Mrs. Calbry, the ceaseless narrative of her esteemed aunt regarding his attachment to Anne, and now his extended stay in Kent puzzled her exceedingly.

Lady Catherine's incessant insistence, combined with Darcy's prolonged stay, kindled the flames of Anne's curiosity, as well. She had grown especially fond of Georgiana over the past months.

Is it possible that we will become sisters? Is that something I truly desire?

I like my cousin well enough—he is handsome and well formed, but he can be haughty and aloof.

He has been somewhat attentive these past weeks, much more than ever, and I do like him.

Nothing would make my mother happier. It would be lovely having Georgiana as a sister, but I do not wish to live anywhere other than Rosings Park.

Pemberley is beautiful, but this is my home. Would he consent to make this his home, as well? Why would he? He loves Pemberley. Might that be a sufficient impediment to an alliance? Would my mother insist that I live at Pemberley solely for the sake of consolidating the two estates?

There came a point when Lady Catherine felt the need to speak with Darcy directly on the matter. Experience had taught her subtlety did not work with the young man, not that she might lay claim to such a talent. She often wondered if her beloved nephew might be suffering some deficit of hearing.

Darcy left the interview with his aunt, thoroughly convincing her ladyship that he also suffered some deficit of speech.

The preponderance of expectancy written on the faces of his aunt, his cousin, his sister, and even the servants was beginning to bore a hole in Darcy's shield of aloofness. He paid homage to his aunt's words while composing a letter to his steward. His silent pondering rendered his efforts futile.

Should I ever agree to such a scheme, it would be with the under-standing of a long engagement, at least four years. Indeed, four years sound reasonable. In fact, why announce any intentions at all? I shall take the next four years to decide.

With that resolution, Darcy made another. It was about time for Georgiana and him to conclude their stay at Rosings Park.

Chapter 20 – Will claim an acquaintance

"**D**ear Charlotte, Thank you for your letter. It comes as such a welcome surprise when I confess to needing it most. I shall be happy to visit with you at your convenience," began Elizabeth's written response to the invitation she had received from one of her oldest friends.

Elizabeth and Charlotte had not stayed in contact with each other as dear friends such as they ought. Elizabeth had disparaged Charlotte's willingness to sacrifice herself to the odious Mr. Collins for the sake of security, and she had made no secret of it.

Nevertheless, Charlotte had tried to reach out to her in support at the prospect of Elizabeth marrying Daniel Calbry. Elizabeth had spurned such attention viewing it akin to pity. Now here Charlotte was reaching out to her again, on the heels of what would have been a horrific scandal for the Bennet family, and a threat to their place amongst the society of Hertfordshire had Mr. Darcy not intervened.

Elizabeth was agreeable towards the scheme. Although she would be a guest in Mr. Collins's home, she would have a much-desired chance to rekindle her friendship with Charlotte, to put another troubling aspect of her past behind.

What if she encountered Mr. Darcy? She knew from Bingley's account that Darcy was now spending more time than not at Rosings Park. Might he still be in Kent when she visited Charlotte? The temptation of seeing him again was too enticing to pass on. He might not love her as he once did, but perhaps they might still be friends.

Friends? In truth, Elizabeth sought more than friendship from Darcy—she even sought more than what she had foolishly proposed to him at Pemberley. Elizabeth thought to have it all ... a friend, a lover, a husband.

Was it too late for a future between them? *Is the reason he now spends so much time in Rosings Park with his cousin a sign he heeded my foolish counsel? Has he decided to offer Miss de Bourgh his hand in marriage?* She must see for herself.

They fixed the date of her arrival and duration of her visit in the next correspondence. Elizabeth was to journey to Hunsford by week's end with a plan to stay a month. Charlotte's remarks spoke of one amongst the party at Rosings Park who would claim an acquaintance with Elizabeth—the gentleman having made Charlotte aware of this of his own accord. Upon first accepting Charlotte's invitation, Elizabeth had done so with a combination of anticipation and dread. She did not fear the possibility of seeing Mr. Darcy. She wanted to. She wanted to see if she still had a chance with him, but she dreaded the possibility that he no longer held her in esteem; even worse, that he had offered for his cousin out of duty, and he might think she was putting herself in his path in visiting a place so near his relations and his presumed intended. News from her friend that Mr. Darcy had spoken with her of their acquaintance was deemed favourable. It increased her hope of seeing him again.

Thus, Elizabeth looked forward to her trip with excitement. A subsequent letter from Charlotte was a splash of cold water on the flames of her hope. It came on the day before her departure. "By the time of your arrival, you will have missed the Darcys. I have learnt from Miss Darcy that her brother and she are to return to Derbyshire. However, we will indeed be a merry party, as we will no doubt have several opportunities to visit with Lady Catherine de Bourgh and her daughter Anne, during your stay. At least, such is my hope. Miss Darcy informed me of her ladyship's anguish over Mr. Darcy's intention not to return to Kent until the spring."

Elizabeth took some comfort from the letter. Charlotte had mentioned both Darcy and Anne with no hint of an attachment. She would not see Darcy, but she would see the woman he might one day marry, allowing her to judge for herself if she should be concerned, jealous, indifferent, or aggrieved. His not being present would allow her to visit his nearest relations and form her own judgements with impunity.

* * *

Every object in the next day's journey was remarkable to Elizabeth. As she drew nearer to Hunsford, she began to think less of Darcy and his relations and more of her own relationship with the Collinses. She had a strong sense of what was expected of her cousin, Mr. Collins—no doubt, he would be eager for her to know all she had missed in rejecting his hand so many years ago, but what might be expected of Charlotte? Having scorned Charlotte for her choice of a husband, she reflected once more on how she had spurned Charlotte's attempts to reach out to her both before and during her marriage to Daniel Calbry. This was not the first time Charlotte had invited her for a visit. Even during her mourning, she had not received Charlotte's condolences as graciously as she should have.

Charlotte and she had grown up together—had considered themselves as the most intimate of friends with a pledge to remain so always. "Does anything last forever?" Elizabeth asked herself aloud, in the seclusion of the carriage. Would the two of them, having grown apart, be able to regain the amity they once shared?

At length, the parsonage was discernible. Mr. Collins and Charlotte appeared at the door, and the carriage stopped at a small gate, which led by a short gravel walk to the house. In a moment, they were all out of the chaise, rejoicing at the sight of each other. Mrs. Collins welcomed her friend with the liveliest pleasure, and Elizabeth was more and more satisfied with coming when she found herself so affectionately received.

She saw her cousin had not changed; his formal civility was what it had been in Hertfordshire, and he detained her some minutes at the gate to receive and satisfy his enquiries after all her family. She was then taken into the house, and he welcomed her a second time with ostentatious formality to his humble abode.

Elizabeth was impressed with the way Charlotte directed their pardon from her husband's company when they almost immediately upon entering the house found themselves seated in a nicely decorated parlour that Charlotte spoke of as reserved for her particular use.

Determined to move past any awkwardness that would be expected after so many years of estrangement, Elizabeth decided the best course of action would be satisfied with an open heart-to-heart talk with her old friend. She spoke of her regret over their long separation; her apology for her role was extended, understood by its recipient, and graciously accepted. In due course, the subject of Elizabeth's sad loss was broached.

"It is only fitting I speak honestly with you on that account," Elizabeth began. "Oh, Charlotte! The truth is I was miserable in my marriage to Daniel Calbry. How many times did you caution me against my unguarded behaviour towards him?"

Elizabeth placed her cup on the side table. She walked towards the window overlooking a pretty garden and wrapped her arms about her shoulders. Charlotte waited. This was not a time for gloating. Elizabeth turned to face her friend.

"Though I did not choose the marriage, but was forced into it, I have been examining the workings of my heart. Who is to say I would not have accepted his hand in marriage had he offered it before I had learnt of his true character? I cannot say in honesty that I would not have agreed to accept his hand—having for a time believed him the best of men. I should have been even more miserable should such have been the case because I would have suffered such shattered dreams and disappointed hopes."

"Dear Eliza, had I known of your suffering, I would not have allowed myself to be so easily persuaded to stay away."

"You could have had no way of knowing—I would not allow anyone to know the truth. My only excuse can be that I felt weary in spirit for so long, yet I was determined to suffer no one's pity. In hindsight, I admit it was a poor excuse for pushing away one as dear to me as you."

"Be that as it may, I am here for you now," Charlotte insisted as she walked over and squeezed her friend's hand.

"Yes, you and Jane, what would I do, if not for the two of you? Moreover, please forgive my ungenerous attitude towards you when you accepted Mr. Collins. I am proud of you. You chose wisely for yourself. You have a comfortable home, a kind husband."

"I am content, as you have imagined. You were always the romantic one. I pray your experience has not turned you against matrimony—that you are open to love, to marrying again, to starting a family," Charlotte voiced, despite her own uneasiness on the subject of children, after years of unsuccessful attempts to bear a child of her own.

"I admit to a time of having given up on love completely, but now I can honestly say I have suffered a complete change of opinion on love, on marriage, and children. I am determined I shall have all that life offers!"

Elizabeth enjoyed the next three days exploring the various paths of the park, identifying her favourites and choosing them as often as possible as an excuse to remain out of doors. Three days had passed with ceaseless talk from Mr. Collins that soon they should expect the honour of an invitation to Rosings from his esteemed patroness.

Elizabeth, too, looked forward to the invitation that did not come. She had heard enough of Lady Catherine to anticipate making her acquaintance with no expectation of a favourable reception, despite Charlotte's insistence to the contrary. Elizabeth had another purpose in mind when considering a visit to Rosings Park, for there was only one touted member of the Rosings household whom she could hardly wait to meet. Elizabeth spoke eagerly of her desire to make acquaintance with Miss Anne de Bourgh. Inwardly, anxiety over meeting the woman perhaps destined to bear the appellation she so carelessly rebuffed weighed heavily.

"Expect to be delighted!" Charlotte exclaimed.

"Delighted?" Elizabeth repeated in doubt. "Unless I am mistaken, she has been described on more than one occasion as being of a frail constitution, timid and withdrawn."

"Indeed, I recall a time when she was rather sickly, thin, and small, but I dare say her constitution, as well as her disposition, have improved over the course of the past weeks—a development attributed to Mr. Darcy's lengthy visit," Charlotte admitted, unsuspectingly distressing her friend. "Although, I have never witnessed anything more than a brotherly regard for Anne from the gentleman, much the same as he attends Miss Darcy, Lady Catherine insists his presence alone accounts for the steady improvement in Anne's health and spirits."

When Mr. Collins could be forgotten, an air of comfort existed throughout the parsonage, and by Charlotte's evident enjoyment of it, Elizabeth supposed he must be often forgotten. When he was about, little else was spoken of other than the invitation to Rosings Park, and when it might come. It was spoken of again at dinner.

"Yes, soon my dear cousin you will have the honour of seeing Lady Catherine de Bourgh," Elizabeth's puffed-up, obsequious cousin observed.

"She is all affability and condescension, as well as a host of other things I need not mention.

"I have little hesitation when I say that she will include you in every invitation with which she honours us during your stay.

"Her behaviour to my dear Charlotte is all that is charming. We dine at Rosings twice every week, which you need not find alarming.

"For we are never allowed to walk home; in that you can trust. Her ladyship's carriage is regularly ordered for us."

Charlotte interrupted her long-winded husband's soliloquy to add, "Lady Catherine is a very respectable, sensible woman and the most attentive neighbour one could ever have."

"True, my dear, that is exactly what I say. I can suppose no greater blessing than to see her each day.

"She is the sort of woman whom one cannot regard with too much deference. I daresay between her ladyship and the king himself, attending to her ladyship is my preference.

"And do not trouble yourself dear cousin, in thinking that the honour she has granted is undeserved. Lady Catherine is no stranger to the meek, though she likes to have the distinction of rank preserved."

At last, the much-anticipated invitation was bestowed. Finally, his dear cousin would be received at her ladyship's grand abode. They had been invited to dine at Rosings Park the next day. Mr. Collins's triumph in consequence of this invitation was complete in every way.

He had long wished for his cousin to witness her ladyship's civility towards himself and his wife. Indeed—this would be one of the most satisfying days of his life. Soon she would know all she had missed in spurning his hand—everything she had disregarded, she would finally understand.

However, of their visit to Rosings for the whole of the next day, Mr. Collins had scarcely anything of worth to say, his remarks sparse in the extreme. He was instructing Elizabeth in what she was to expect, for surely the sight of such rooms, so many servants, and so splendid a dinner would be more than she could suspect.

"I would advise you merely to put on whichever of your clothes is superior to the rest. Lady Catherine will not think the worse of you for being simply dressed."

While she was dressing, he came two or three times to her door—be quick, he would remind her, stating it unpardonable to keep Lady Catherine waiting for her dinner.

Good heavens! Elizabeth silently screamed, as much amused as she was offended. Entertaining a sycophant like her cousin at least twice a week could not bode well for her ladyship. Esteemed by her nephew, sister of his beloved mother, mother of his supposed intended; finally, she would see what all the fuss was about.

Chapter 21 – My share of the conversation

When they ascended the steps to the hall, Elizabeth made note of the distinct contrast of Rosings to Pemberley, the former ornate and ostentatious, designed to inspire awe more than to welcome. The three of them followed the servant through an antechamber. Undaunted by the grandeur surrounding her, Elizabeth found she was equal to the scene and able to observe the ladies before her composedly. After examining the mother, in whose countenance and deportment she soon found some resemblance to Mr. Darcy, she turned her eyes on the daughter. She joined in Charlotte's assessment of her being of warm complexion and good health, even if rather thin and small. Elizabeth perceived her a delightful creature.

Her ladyship, with pronounced condescension, arose to receive them, "So, you are Mrs. Elizabeth Calbry."

"I am your ladyship. I am honoured to make your acquaintance."

"Charming—this is my daughter, Anne." Anne nodded. Elizabeth curtsied.

With the attention of his patroness diverted, Collins remarked to Elizabeth about the many superb features of the room. She paid him little mind. A faint sound drew her eyes to the door. She commanded her heart to be still as she stared at the embodiment of all her most recent dreams.

"Mr. Darcy?"

"Mrs. Calbry," Darcy responded with a bow.

Elizabeth reminded herself to curtsy. "Sir—"

Mr. Collins stepped in front of her, cutting off her speech. He cowered under the infamous Darcy mien. Darcy read in Elizabeth's eyes the question of his being there.

"Mrs. Calbry, I am a guest here."

Lady Catherine remarked, "Of course, you had already met my nephew in Hertfordshire, no doubt, when he visited Charles Bingley earlier this year."

"Yes, you are correct, your ladyship."

Soon, a short, plain-looking gentleman entered the room and stood next to Darcy. His eyes fixed upon Elizabeth, though he directed his speech to Darcy.

"I say, old fellow, will you not introduce me?"

As if I have a choice, Darcy considered.

Tossing decorum aside, the gentleman reached for Elizabeth's hand. "Colonel Richard Fitzwilliam, at your service, my lady." He bowed and bestowed a light kiss across her knuckles. Darcy fought to keep from rolling his eyes.

* * *

With everyone assembled, Lady Catherine questioned the wisdom of proceeding with the evening's plans. Her ladyship was not at all comfortable having either of her nephews in the company of Mrs. Calbry. She had her own ideas on the temptations a beautiful young widow might present. She wanted them to have nothing to do with her. Yet, with the invitation, extended and accepted, and her nephews arrived so unexpectedly, what else might she do but make the most of it? Not that she was above rescinding the invitation at the last minute, but her curiosity to meet the young woman begged to be satisfied.

Darcy questioned his decision to drag his cousin to Rosings Park with him. Contriving to be seated next to Elizabeth, the colonel attended to her with the easiness of a long-time acquaintance. His uncanny familiarity with her caused her to wonder if Darcy had spoken of her to the gentleman.

Unable to think of anything beyond Darcy's sudden appearance, she silently conjectured. *Now I shall determine what he is about. I shall know in an instant if he has formed an attachment with his cousin—if his heart has hardened against me.* If she were to rely purely upon his countenance to know how he felt, she would be disappointed, for his face bore the imperturbable mask she associated with the days of their earliest acquaintance.

Lady Catherine accounted for Darcy's unexpected return to Rosings Park as a sign of his increasing devotion to Anne. Distraught as she had become over his abrupt departure less than a week prior, she was now elated with his even more impulsive return.

After a brief interlude, dinner was announced, and everyone proceeded into the dining room. Darcy was obliged to escort his aunt and cousin, Mr. Collins escorted his dear wife, and Richard had the honour of escorting Elizabeth. After some mix-up with the seating arrangements that vexed Lady Catherine exceedingly, she decreed Mr. Collins was not to sit next to his wife, a declaration that resulted in Elizabeth taking the seat next to Darcy.

Thus, an awkward dinner ensued, at least for Darcy. There was no hiding Darcy's unease. His first opportunity to see Elizabeth since they were together at Pemberley, and he found himself seated within inches of her. Distracted by her fragrance, his mind drifted off in recollection of their last night together.

Elizabeth noticed his increasing discomfiture. Her own composure suffered a similar disturbance. Darcy could only wish that the consequence of several courses of dinner, along with his aunt's appreciation of her own voice would afford him much-needed time to adjust himself to being so close to Elizabeth again.

"Darcy, have you heard one word I have said?" Lady Catherine had posed the question on the health of his sister twice.

Darcy looked at her in puzzlement.

Richard intervened on his cousin's behalf. "Georgiana is quite well, Lady Catherine."

That served to bring Darcy's attention back to the present. "Might I inquire of the health of your family, Mrs. Calbry?"

Elizabeth longed for a moment alone with him, to apologise for her intrusion upon his family. Making the most of the somewhat awkward turn of events, she responded, "They are very well. Thank you for asking."

"How have you been ... since we last met?"

"As well as can be expected, I should imagine." Elizabeth placed her silverware aside and gave Darcy her full attention. "I had no idea you would be here. I was informed you had returned to Pemberley."

"Actually, I have been in Matlock with Georgiana and my uncle and aunt. This trip came about ... unexpectedly."

"Oh!" she replied in wonderment. "Will you be staying long in Kent?"

"I do not know. That is to say—my plans remain unfixed. It all depends."

"What are you and Mrs. Calbry speaking of, Nephew?" Lady Catherine interrupted. "I must have my share of the conversation."

Two courses into the dinner, Elizabeth considered that whilst Anne, who sat directly across the elegantly arranged table from Darcy, often looked upon him with a special regard, she could not detect any particular regard from Darcy towards Anne, except as Charlotte had described it—that of brotherly concern. He rarely spoke to his cousin at all, but Elizabeth could not use that as any sort of confirmation, as he had barely spoken to anyone during the meal, including herself.

After dinner, Lady Catherine grew weary of what she perceived as odd behaviour on Darcy's part. She chastised him more than once to attend to her conversation, to stop pacing the room, to come away from the window, and to take a seat beside Anne. Richard was delighted to have the pleasure of Elizabeth's company. He monopolised her the entire evening. Darcy had never been more frustrated than he was that evening, again wondering why he had brought Richard along and what if anything he might do to send him on his way ... alone.

Darcy had missed Elizabeth so much. He dared not visit his friend Bingley at his home in Hertfordshire—her home. He doubted his ability to stick to his resolve to meet her disaffectedly. And yet he found himself, the same day of having learnt from his aunt that she was visiting her friend in Hunsford, commanding his cousin immediately (with no regard for any plans that might have been in conflict with his own), to accompany him to Kent, less than a week since Georgiana and he last departed. Darcy believed it was safe to encounter her again in Kent, where temptation might be resisted amongst the bosom of his family. As the Darcys had been visiting the Fitzwilliams at their country home at the time, Georgiana was to remain in Matlock in their relatives' care.

Darcy was more than happy when the carriage was called to convey the Hunsford party to the parsonage. In a bold and calculating move, he managed to outmanoeuvre Richard and handed Elizabeth into the carriage himself. The fact that he escorted the Hunsford party to the awaiting carriage at all, prompted strange stares from his aunt upon his return to the drawing room, but she said not a word. Lady Catherine was not the only person to take note of Darcy's unusual behaviour; at least two others had questioned his peculiar state, as well.

Darcy's gesture did little to reassure Elizabeth. *He was merely acting the part of a gentleman,* she said to herself. *A servant or even Mr. Collins might just as well have assisted me.*

* * *

Elizabeth stayed up late. What little sleep she managed was fitful, as she allowed her reflections on the events of the evening to rob her of her slumber. She had often wondered how it would be when they met again. Would they meet without intolerable embarrassment over their one night of shared passion? Would he be angry with her still for her rejection of his marriage proposal? Would he remain her intimate friend? Were other nights of passion in their future?

Alas, no answers had been forthcoming. Her list of questions only grew. They had met, and she knew not where she stood with him. A bow, a curtsy, one long insufferable meal. *Was he angry ... discouraged or displeased?*

She longed to reach out to him, to touch him, and to be touched by him. Did he feel the same? *I have used him ill and disappointed him. He has not forgiven me.*

The late night silence concocted enough suppositions to fill Elizabeth's bedchamber.

How disappointed he must have been to find me, of all people, at Rosings Park, of all places. He is lost to me. Things will never be the same.

Now we are strangers, no—we are worse than strangers.

The next morning, Elizabeth returned to the parsonage after her customary walk, in time to enjoy breakfast with Charlotte. For the first time since her arrival, Mr. Collins was out and about the first thing in the morning, attending to his parishioners.

"Tell me, dear Eliza, how well do Mr. Darcy and you know each other?" Charlotte inquired, causing Elizabeth to suspect that perhaps Charlotte had planned her husband's absence.

"Charlotte, what kind of question is that?"

"One that deserves an honest answer. Mr. Darcy had told me of your acquaintance from Hertfordshire; however, I am wondering if it is more than a casual acquaintance. He stared at you most of the evening. I might add that his increasing discomfort was difficult to ignore." Charlotte smirked. "It is little wonder he was unable to sit still."

Elizabeth coloured. "You attribute THAT to my presence!"

"I have spent enough evenings with the gentleman to attest that it is something I have never detected prior to last evening."

"Charlotte! You should not be speaking of such things."

"And why should I not? We are not maidens, after all. Now, tell me the truth about your acquaintance with Mr. Darcy."

"Charlotte, I fear you may think me foolish if I confess the entirety of my history with the gentleman to you."

"Of course I would not ... that is unless you say he offered you marriage and you rejected his proposal."

Elizabeth coloured. She remembered why she kept her dear friend at a distance for so long. *Have I ever been able to hide anything from Charlotte?* She spoke not a word.

"No!" Charlotte threw her hands in the air. "What were you thinking?"

"Charlotte, I have been so blind—" she began. Elizabeth did not tell her friend all that she had experienced with Darcy over the past months, but she did confess that they had become intimate friends, had indeed fallen in love, and that she rejected his proposal at a time when she had given up on marriage, to say nothing at all of love.

"Nevertheless, as you can see for yourself, he may spend a great deal of time looking at me, something he has always done, mind you. However, I have wounded him, and if his behaviour last evening is any indication, he means to make certain that it never happens again."

"There—I believe you are wrong. I think he is in danger of doing anything you ask of him, my dear Eliza."

If only you knew.

Chapter 22 – This piece of civility

S oon after breakfast, Charlotte and Elizabeth sat in the parlour side by side, perusing a fashion magazine Elizabeth had brought along on her visit. Two distinguished gentleman callers walked into the room.

The difference between the two was pronounced. One tall, handsome, brooding, and determined to be silent; the other not attractive in appearance, but gregarious and loquacious and determined to be agreeable.

Charlotte tried to draw the colonel's attention away from Elizabeth, thinking perhaps that Mr. Darcy would seize the opportunity to speak with her. It had yet to happen. Richard was fascinated with Elizabeth. Every answer to one of Charlotte's inquiries was followed up with, "What say you, Mrs. Calbry." "Perhaps we should ask Mrs. Calbry ..." Mrs. Calbry this and Mrs. Calbry that.

Fortunately, the less restrictive society of Hunsford allowed for a much longer morning call than one might expect in town. After a while, even Richard ran out of witty and charming things to say, thus providing an opening for Elizabeth and Darcy to talk. He moved to a seat closer to her.

"Are you enjoying your stay, Mrs. Calbry?"

She answered him in the usual way and after a moment's hesitation, added, "Might I ask why you choose to refer to me by my late husband's surname? I believe we are long past such formalities, or are we now to behave as indifferent acquaintances?"

"Under the circumstances—" he started.

"To what circumstances are you referring, Mr. Darcy?"

"I," Darcy attempted, but was unable to continue in light of the unexpected turn of events.

Mr. Collins rushed into the room, completely out of breath, as he had been far away when word of the eminent visitors to the parsonage reached his hearing.

"I beg your pardons, Mr. Darcy, Colonel Fitzwilliam. Welcome to my humble abode. Forgive me for tarrying about while you were forced to wait. I had no idea to expect you might call, as we are all to dine again at Rosings in but three days."

"Do not be uneasy, sir. We were obliged to call upon Mrs. Collins and her guest. You need not have bothered to rush all the way home," said Richard. "For Heaven's sake, sit down and catch your breath."

"It is no bother at all. I am proud to receive the distinguished nephews of my esteemed patroness in my home. I fear I would be remiss in my duties not to attend you. My dear wife and I are honoured indeed. Mrs. Collins, have you offered the gentlemen refreshments?"

"I have, Mr. Collins."

"Yes—yes. I see. May I fetch either of you anything more? I am at your service."

"No—actually, we are about to leave," Darcy said as he stood to address Charlotte. "Mrs. Collins, Mrs.—" he cut off his parting words and bowed to both ladies. "It was nice seeing you. Good day."

Darcy and Richard left with Mr. Collins on their heels, promising to remain at home every morning for the rest of their stay, so they would be sure not to miss one another again. Once more, he offered profuse apologies for not having received them properly upon their arrival.

As Darcy left the parsonage with few words exchanged between them, Elizabeth was struck with the feeling of the two of them being lost to each other. *Why had he called at all if he meant to remain silent and taciturn?*

What might have happened had Mr. Collins not interrupted? He alluded to circumstances. What circumstances?

Charlotte interrupted Elizabeth's reverie with her opinion of how the morning's enjoyment of the illustrious visitors at the parsonage came to be.

"I may thank you, Eliza, for this piece of civility. Mr. Darcy has never taken the opportunity to call upon me in the past, despite overwhelming opportunities to do so with the amount of time he has spent in Kent in recent weeks."

"I dare not refute your assertion, dear Charlotte. Surely, you have intimate knowledge of Mr. Darcy's habits in that regard. However, how do you reconcile his behaviour?"

"Perhaps, you might give Mr. Darcy the benefit of the doubt. Can you imagine someone with his bent getting a word in edgewise against the colonel?"

Elizabeth acknowledged her friend's sentiments with a faint smile. She had her own thoughts on the matter. She begged Charlotte's pardon and ventured out of doors for a solitary walk to recover her spirits, or in other words, to dwell without interruption on those subjects that must deaden them more. Mr. Darcy's behaviour astonished and vexed her.

Why, if he came only to remain grave and indifferent, did he come at all? She could settle it in no way that gave her pleasure. *I know him well enough to know he can be amiable and pleasing when he chooses. If he no longer cares for me, why silence? Teasing, teasing, man! I shall not think about him.*

She thought of little else. *What are the circumstances he speaks of? Is it my refusal of his hand? What else might it be? A man who has once been refused! What a fool I am to expect a renewal of his love? What gentleman would not protest against such a weakness as a second proposal to the same woman?*

Discouraged by her disregard for him, their encounter frustrated Darcy, as well. Every smile Elizabeth had bestowed upon the colonel had caused Darcy to wish even more that he had left him in Matlock. Darcy wished there had been more time to speak with her that morning. Too much was unsaid between them. What had she thought of the letter? Did she find his manner to be too presumptuous? Again? How might he even broach the subject without chancing the opening of wounds not yet healed? Even with the ability to see her again, to spend time in her company—he still smarted from her rejection of his hand in marriage, the only woman in the world to whom he had given his heart and pledged his troth. He wished for any indication that she might have changed her mind. He detected none at all.

The next couple of days did not see a return of the gentlemen to the parsonage. They did not call. Elizabeth found her spirits in flux with a sense of melancholy always pervading. She suffered listlessness, weariness. No matter how much she determined to think about anything else, thoughts of the time spent at Pemberley with Darcy always prevailed.

Now he was just across the park; he might as well have been one thousand miles away.

On a subsequent morning, the colonel arrived at the parsonage alone. Elizabeth considered the worst. Mr. Darcy was so disinterested, he did not bother to call. Deciding to take Richard up on his invitation for a walk, she donned her bonnet, and they sat out on one of her favourite paths.

"Darcy tells me that you visited Pemberley this summer. Tell me —what do you think of his home?"

"Pemberley is quite wonderful. Never have I seen a place for which nature has done more. The manor is magnificent, the woods are beautiful, and the paths are the most enchanting I have seen."

"I shall not argue with you. I enjoy Pemberley much the same as I enjoy my parents' home."

"Indeed. What else did Mr. Darcy tell you, other than that I was his guest?"

"Nothing of importance, to be sure."

"Does Mr. Darcy remain at Rosings this morning?"

"Yes—he is occupied by some estate business on Lady Catherine's behalf."

"Oh! Yes," Elizabeth said dryly. "Mr. Darcy takes his responsibilities to his family seriously, I suppose."

"Indeed, he does. In matters regarding Pemberley, as well as Rosings Park, he is most diligent. Of course, he has been quite torn over the extent of those duties of late."

"What do you mean?"

"It is a circumstance which Darcy, of course, would not wish known. This is a sensitive matter where our family is concerned."

"You may depend upon my not mentioning it."

"Darcy stands to gain all of Rosings Park should he honour his duty to his family and marry Anne. Although I can safely say, the matter has not been at the forefront of his mind—till lately, that is. He has spent much time at Rosings, deciding if his future is indeed with Anne."

"Did Mr. Darcy tell you this—that he is considering marrying his cousin?"

"No, it is total conjecture on my part. I know him. I know of no other reason he insisted we rush to Kent, only days after his departure. He spends more time with Anne than ever before. After all, was it not the Roman poet Sextus Propertius who rendered, 'always toward absent lovers love's tide stronger flows'?"

This was spoken jestingly, but the words painted so apt a picture of Mr. Darcy's behaviour that she would not trust herself with an answer; and, therefore, abruptly changing the conversation, talked on indifferent matters until they reached the parsonage.

Meanwhile, Darcy and Anne enjoyed a leisurely stroll along another lane of Rosings Park, as they had done daily since his return.

"I must say, it was such a relief finally to meet the third party of our companionship of these past weeks," Anne said, breaking the silence that began the moment they had left the manor house.

"I am afraid I do not take your meaning, Anne," Darcy responded, too perplexed to respond in a more forthcoming manner.

"For weeks, you have attended me most consistently—looking without seeing, listening without hearing and speaking without saying anything."

"Oh, pardon me," said Darcy, oblivious of whatever his cousin was saying. The two of them walked along in silence for a few moments longer until Anne was compelled to speak again.

"Are you in love?"

He heard that!

With speed akin to a flash of lighting tracking across the sky, Darcy began to recount all his recent encounters with his cousin. *Have I been in any way unguarded in my attentions towards Anne? Of course, I love her, she is my family, but I am not in love with her. Have my frequent visits to Rosings Park, of late, increased her expectations? Does she expect an offer of marriage?*

While Elizabeth had thought a lot of Anne over the past weeks, so had Anne thought of Elizabeth, especially of late. Elizabeth's reputation had preceded her. Georgiana, while in the company of Mrs. Collins, occasionally had spoken of her. Anne suspected more to Darcy's "friendship" with Mrs. Elizabeth Calbry than Georgiana was willing to share. She knew they had first met in Hertfordshire. It was not inconceivable that their paths had crossed in town. However, Georgiana had not mentioned a word of her being a guest at Pemberley, leading Anne to wonder why. Richard had been the one to enlighten her of the facts.

Her question yet unanswered, Anne scrutinised her cousin. Poor Fitzwilliam! She likened his countenance to that of a defenceless animal caught in a trap. She understood her cousin too well to suffer any doubt of where his thoughts tended. She did not allow him to suffer too long.

"Fitzwilliam, please, take a deep breath. I do not fancy that you are in love with me. I speak of your obvious admiration of Mrs. Calbry. What I am asking is, are you in love with her?"

Startled, he had no idea what he might say. *Is my love for Elizabeth that obvious?*

"Your silence is confirmation enough. If you love her, why are you wasting your time with me? I advise you to follow your heart."

"It is not as simple as you suggest."

"What prohibits you? Surely, it is not her lack of wealth or connections. She is a gentleman's daughter, is she not?"

"It is not that."

"It cannot be that she was once married. She is alone now. I dare say she possesses a liveliness of spirit ideally suited to the taciturn bent of yours."

"It is complicated, Anne. Something I find myself unable to explain."

"Whatever the impediment, it is obvious that you love her, and I believe she shares your sentiments. I beg of you, do not think you are bound to me owing to some out-dated notion of familial duty. You owe me nothing."

Darcy stood before his cousin and rested both hands on her arms. The last thing he would ever want to do is hurt her. "Is that how you truly feel, Anne? Do you truly believe that anything more between us would only result from a sense of duty on my part?"

Anne returned Darcy's probing gaze with one of her own. She had offered him exactly what he wanted most—a release from their mothers' preconceived notions of their destiny, despite the pain and sacrifice to herself, which she would admit to no one. Yet, he now questioned her intent. She wondered what he was about.

Chapter 23 – *Taught me to hope*

Anne's talk with Darcy did not go as she had expected. Upon her return to the house, she sought her cousin Richard straightaway. The two engaged in a lengthy *tête-à-tête*, the subject of which, one can only imagine, but they remained close by each other for the remainder of the afternoon while entertaining the Hunsford party.

Richard waited for the right moment before speaking of a topic that was sure to affect the sensibilities of his aunt ... one of a young gentleman who had recently married.

"Young Mr. Dunsmore married, did you say? What with his family's wealth and the expectations attuned to the young man's status, I should imagine his bride is a young lady from a family of large fortune." Her ladyship raised her fan. "Is the young lady's family known to us?"

"I dare say they are not. Nevertheless, she is a lovely creature. The daughter of a gentleman from Somersetshire with little wealth to speak of save a comfortable estate, I hear."

"Why, I never!" Shocked and astonished, Lady Catherine exclaimed, "Do you mean to say the young woman dared to aspire to a situation in life beyond that in which she was reared. What must his parents think?"

Little chance Elizabeth would hold her tongue thinking as she did on the subject. In her arguments put forth to her ladyship, Elizabeth refuted many of the opinions she had espoused, hurling them at Darcy only months ago, in rejecting his marriage proposal. At length, Lady Catherine thought to put a stop to such impertinent nonsense.

"Mrs. Calbry gives her opinion most decidedly," said Lady Catherine to no one in particular. "Nevertheless, I shall persist in my superior contention that one should not aspire to marry beyond the sphere to which they have been born."

Elizabeth spoke again. "Both the lady in question and the gentleman are of the same sphere despite the disparity of their fortunes. He is a gentleman; she is a gentleman's daughter. That makes them equal. The two of them have chosen happiness regardless of society's strictures. I should imagine they only resolved to act in a manner which would constitute their own happiness, without reference to anyone so wholly unconnected with them."

Elizabeth's words cast a pall over the room. Lady Catherine especially was taken aback by her impudence. Charlotte was aghast. Darcy was baffled.

Did she say—despite the disparity in fortune, the two had chosen happiness?

After having instigated the scene purposely, Richard was content to settle back in his seat and observe.

Suspicion reared its head. It had hardly escaped Lady Catherine's notice that Darcy appeared more interested in this young woman than he dared to show. His sudden return to Rosings Park without an offer of marriage to Anne could mean only one thing!

"I should imagine happiness in marriage is of no consequence when considered from the grander scheme of upholding society's conventions."

Elizabeth rose to her ladyship's challenge. "I contend happiness in marriage is of the greatest consequence. As the lady is indeed a gentleman's daughter, then surely, they must be considered equals. Given a true meeting of the minds, nothing should stand in the way of their happiness, neither rank nor privilege, neither status nor even age, I dare say."

Darcy furrowed his eyebrow. *Did she say—even age?*

"Why, I never heard such a thing! Young people should honour the traditions of their parents and only marry those of equal consequence. It is such a blessing to know my Anne will soon be married to my own dear nephew Darcy," she opined confidently without acknowledging either of the two young people.

156   P O Dixon

"Darcy has been most attentive in his courtship of my Anne these past weeks. It can only be a short time before he makes their attachment official; I am certain of it."

Lady Catherine persisted in talking at length of the pending union, as if it had been announced in *The Morning Post*, while Darcy sat in studied indifference, quite oblivious of his aunt, lost in contemplation of Elizabeth's speech.

Darcy was no more tuned to his aunt's nattering that afternoon than any other. As usual, his countenance betrayed no awareness she was engaged in any manner of discourse at all. Elizabeth observed the impenetrable Darcy mask and knew not what to suppose. Surely, he was aware his aunt had practically announced his engagement to her daughter.

Elizabeth searched Darcy's face to ascertain his reaction to his aunt's pronouncement. She saw for once that he was not looking at her. Nor was he looking at Anne or his aunt. Instead, he was staring off into the distance.

Lady Catherine speaks the truth!

Elizabeth's hands trembled. The rattling of her cup when she returned it to her saucer would have awakened the dead. Perturbed and distressed, Elizabeth abruptly rose.

"Pardon me, your ladyship."

Before Lady Catherine could respond, Elizabeth raced from the room, Charlotte on her heels. Elizabeth braced herself against the wall to reclaim her composure. Charlotte's unexpected attendance startled her.

"Dear Lizzy, are you quite all right?"

"Yes! Oh Charlotte, I hardly know what to feel. I simply needed to escape. I shall scream if I have to hear another account of Miss de Bourgh's excellent fortune."

"I understand exactly how you must be feeling, my dear. I cannot account for Mr. Darcy being so obtuse just now. I know he does not love Anne, as I am sure he is in love with you. However, I can no longer discredit Lady Catherine's claim if the gentleman will not do so himself.

"Do not fret. I will make your excuses. However, are you certain you wish to walk? Lady Catherine would not object to having the carriage called for."

"Absolutely not. I love to walk, as you know. The fresh air will serve me well. Enjoy your visit and do not make yourself uneasy over me. I shall be fine. I simply require time to myself. I will see you later this evening."

Mr. Collins was too embarrassed by Elizabeth's ill-mannered behaviour towards his esteemed patroness to worry about her abrupt departure. In light of the slight to her ladyship, and to him by default, he was secretly delighted when Charlotte returned to the drawing room alone.

In her haste to escape Rosings, Elizabeth was careless. Instead of heading directly to the parsonage, she wandered about aimlessly and did not detect the dark clouds quickly moving across the horizon. She soon recognized her error and, even sooner than she would have imagined, buckets of pounding rain poured from the sky.

Amidst the torrential downfall, she raced across the bridge seeking refuge in a massive stone temple, reminiscent of something from a distant land, another place and time, just ahead.

Shelter at last, she thought. She rested her head against the solid rock wall. She wiped the streams of raindrops that trickled down her face from the brim of her drenched bonnet.

I am sure to catch my death of cold. However, I would rather be here than back in the stifling confines of Rosings. Clutching her thoroughly soaked bonnet in one hand, she had barely calmed herself when his approach shook her senses. She gasped aloud! From nowhere, he stood before her, as dripping wet as she was.

The chaotic forces of the wind, the thunderous roar of nearby lightning strikes, loomed as faint as whispers compared with the pounding in her chest. A long silence ensued; each took the measure of the other.

Why is he here?

When Mrs. Collins returned to the drawing room alone, it finally had dawned upon Darcy how Elizabeth might have perceived his silence in response to his aunt's ramblings. He immediately excused himself from the party with the intention of once and for all clearing the air between the two of them. The sudden, violent storm in which he found himself, struck him with a deep sense of anxiety that she might be wandering around alone, with no protection. He thanked God he had found her safe and unharmed.

Darcy approached Elizabeth. He touched her face, her hair, partly to reassure himself that she was all right, but mostly to feel the soft delicacy of her skin once more. The estranged lovers stood at a precipice.

Though their eyes met with uncertainty, their lips parted with anticipation. As close as two people could be, at last, their willing lips combined. Both sensed it—panic felt moments before now replaced by visceral calm only found in the warmth of each other.

Elizabeth pulled away. "What are you doing? You are betrothed!"

"No—no, I am not."

"Your cousin ... Anne—Lady Catherine announced your intention to marry Anne. You did not deny it. You said nothing to contradict her!"

"I am here with you."

"Which signifies what?"

"It signifies that I love you. I love you. I love you now as much as ever. Elizabeth, you have bewitched me—mind, body, and soul. I cannot bear to go on without you. These past months have been a torment. I came back to Rosings for the sole object of seeing you. I had to see you."

He reclaimed her in his arms. Then he placed his hand on her cheek. "Your words spoken back there, to my aunt, have taught me to hope as I scarcely allowed myself before." Kissing her upon her forehead, he pleaded, "Tell me your feelings are the same as mine ... that you love and need me as much as I do you. Let me live the rest of my life loving you ... as my wife."

He kissed her. "Will you let me?"

Darcy prayed Elizabeth would not renew her proposal to be his mistress, knowing if she did, he would be compelled to say yes. He so loved this woman.

Elizabeth silently thanked God that Darcy had renewed his offer of marriage, knowing if he now were contented simply to be her lover, she would be compelled to say no. She so loved this man.

"Mr. Darcy, the feelings you have expressed so affectionately represent my own sentiments. The words you have spoken are exactly those I had convinced myself that I might never hear again. I hardly know what to say." Remnants of raindrops dripping from her hair masked her tears.

"Say yes."

"Yes!"

The rain was still crashing down around them, even heavier now and made worse by the gusting winds. The warmth of his smile caused her to forget she was soaking wet and chilled through and through. Blissful moments drifted in impassioned silence. Neither of the two lovers wanted to be the first to speak, the first to break the magical spell cast about them. Alas, it must be so. Elizabeth was not nearly as heavily attired as was Darcy. He needed to take care of her.

Darcy's strong arms protected her, sheltered her from the storm. His soft, soothing words embraced Elizabeth, letting her know she was safe. She was where she belonged.

With no precise measure of how long the two held on to each other, the storm abated, bestowing a marvellous double rainbow across the clearing sky and faintly reflecting in the pond. Elizabeth witnessed her surroundings and silently rejoiced.

Heaven must be like this.

She said yes! Darcy opened his eyes and witnessed the beautiful late afternoon unfolding around them. It was a dream coming true. He smiled. *This must be heaven!*

He kissed Elizabeth softly upon her forehead. "Let us get you out of these wet clothes."

"I know we should take this opportunity to escape to a place where it is warm and dry, but I do not want us to part just yet."

"Then, I will not leave you ... come with me."

He would get no objection. Neither propriety nor decorum would stop her from following him wherever he might lead. He took her hand and led her along a path he claimed rarely used by anyone but him, a secret path—one that might deliver them to their destination with alacrity. That was but one beauty of the path, the other being its relative seclusion, which allowed Darcy to sweep Elizabeth up into his arms and carry her the remainder of the way. With little concern for discovery, he spoke to her of his anguish over their separation and his joyous anticipation of their future, all while bestowing tender kisses liberally about her face.

Darcy followed the shortest route he knew and soon led Elizabeth up to the gate and through the door of the parsonage, amidst light streams of protest that they might be seen. Pulling her forward by the hand, he said,

"Will you calm yourself—and what if we are detected? The ensuing scandal would only dictate we marry immediately."

"I find the prospect of a scandalous marriage not at all amusing. If you will recall, I have travelled that route before. I do not wish to follow that path again, not even for you, sir."

"Of course not, my love. That was insensitive of me. Forgive me."

"Perhaps this once."

"Thank you. As for any gossip our being here alone might give rise to, I will have my man purchase all the servants' silence, if need be. I should be able to silence them until after the wedding, at least.

"Dinner at Rosings will last for hours, as you well know. The evening is ours."

"Do you not think your presence will be missed?"

"I have no doubt. However, Richard should suffer no difficulty in preventing my aunt from organising a search party. Now, hurry upstairs and out of those wet clothes. I shall remain the perfect gentleman and await your return."

"Well, Mr. Darcy ... as long as you intend to buy everyone's silence, you might as well get your money's worth," she said as she refused to release his hand and led him towards the stairway.

Elizabeth went directly behind the dressing screen in her room and began removing her wet clothes. Having not retrieved a fresh nightgown, she directed Darcy to perform the task for her. Darcy took a break from tending the fire and heeded her command. That duty he found diverting; as he sorted through her things, a variety of cottons and muslins, he noted not a silk or satin negligee amongst them. Disappointed, he selected a nightgown that might readily be removed should the need arise.

Elizabeth emerged from behind the screen. Darcy had removed his wet clothing, as well, all except his shirt and pants. He sat on the bed with her and began drying her hair with a towel.

"I have yet to comprehend the history of how your marriage came about. I would like to know the whole story."

"And you will soon, I promise. However, let us not spoil this wonderful day speaking of those not so pleasant aspects of the past."

"Whenever you are ready, I will be here." Darcy decided not to press, certain she would open up to him in time. Though he sensed she was still grappling with a few concerns, he felt all was well between them. With his help, they would work through her worries together.

They discussed noteworthy matters that had occurred during their months apart. For Elizabeth, Jane's support had been a godsend as had been Charlotte's, but the time with Darcy at the end of the Season and the months spent with him at Pemberley had been the basis for something even more imperative. Darcy had become Elizabeth's closest friend and she, his. They had missed each other and the intimacy of their conversations.

He had not been mistaken in the words of his letter. She had failed to come to grips with her past, to accept it for what it had been ... to let go. She placed her hand in his and said,

"You sir, are a dream come true. I should imagine that I have been waiting for you all my life, and I never even knew it. I certainly was not looking for anyone—though my existence was uninhabited before you came into it, I was content to remain as I was forever. Thank you for your love."

"I should be thanking you ... for allowing me to love you."

"Your letter forced me to face my past and put it behind me. I am sorry I pushed you away." On a lighter note, she continued, "Then again, I suppose I should be upset with you for allowing me to believe I had no chance when you showed up here."

The purpose of his lengthy visit to Kent over the summer, his attentions towards his cousin, the disregard for his aunt's insistence that Anne and he marry ... he addressed without qualification or reserve. Yes—he had considered whether his future lay with his cousin. Indeed, he had endeavoured to learn to be indifferent.

"Did you expect me to wait forever for you to change your mind about us?"

Darcy darted, escaping a pillow spiralling towards his head. "I most certainly did."

"And I would have—so there," he confided cheekily, but soon added, "for at least four to five years."

Dodging a second pillow, the little-boy smile that graced his face proved too hard to resist. She let his taunt pass without further retaliation, leaned forward and kissed his cheek. He had weighed his love for her against his duty to his family and chosen her—even to wait for her. That was cause for neither repine nor reproach; it was a cause for gladness.

Some mention of his role in her sister's recovery was unavoidable.

"You must allow me to thank you for everything you did to recover my youngest sister, Mr. Darcy."

"How did you learn of my involvement?"

"Why, Jane of course! Did you truly believe Charles would not confide in Jane—that she would not confide in me?"

"I suppose I had hoped to keep my role a secret. I did not do it for anyone's gratitude."

"Then, why did you do it?"

"Surely, you must know. I did it for you. I wished to spare you the heartache and pain of having a sister lost to you and your family. You must know I will do everything that is in my power to ensure your happiness."

"But I must express my gratitude. Moreover, I must ask you, for I cannot help wondering how you bear the thought of George Wickham as a brother-in-law. Surely, the prospect must grieve you."

"Indeed, however, it would be nothing in comparison to the pain and grief I would suffer in not having you as my wife. He is in Newcastle, and God willing, we shall never cross paths with him again. This is not to say that you should not see your sister. She will always be welcomed in our home. Her husband never will be."

Elizabeth saw no point in belabouring the point. In time, he might change his mind.

Once warm and dry, Elizabeth made her way to the kitchen to gather what she could in the way of bread, assorted fruit, and cheese. She had spent enough time in that very room with Charlotte to know her way around. She soon loaded her small bounty into a basket, along with a bottle of wine and glasses. Darcy had removed the soft bed covers and pillows and placed them on the floor in front of the fireplace while she was downstairs. Once Elizabeth arranged their meal, Darcy lay down and rested his head in her lap. As she stroked his soft hair and fed him bits of food, Darcy comforted himself with the thought that it should always be that way.

"You should know this is the sort of thing I expect when we are married."

"Oh, you do! Do you suppose I shall be that kind of wife? One who submits to your will—one who always does as you bid. I have to say I should hope not. I hope you know me better than that. Otherwise, you would soon grow miserable with such an impudent wife—you might lavish your discontent upon me. Then where would we be?"

"My beautiful Elizabeth—you are the most nonsensical woman, at times. I know you well enough not to attempt to reign in that impudence of yours, even should I wish it. I shall save myself the trouble and not even try," he teased.

"You know that I speak in jest. Your spirit, your wit, and I dare say your impertinence combine to increase my love for you. I have no wish to change you. I love everything about you."

"I was hardly in doubt that you loved me once, though I must confess I grew less and less convinced of your constancy once I saw you again."

To his puzzled expression, she replied, "Why so silent and taciturn? I was afraid your interest had waned. What made you so shy of me, when we first met at Rosings? Why, especially did you look as if you did not care about me?"

"Because, you showed such liveliness and cheer with my cousin, but towards me, you were silent and demur. You gave me no encouragement."

"But I was embarrassed over what had occurred between us at Pemberley. I was afraid you had not forgiven me."

"So was I."

"Then, your silence the next morning, here at the parsonage, was insufferable. Why did you show such unwillingness to speak to me when you arrived?"

"A man who had felt less, might have said more. Is not my cousin Richard a fitting example? Would you prefer I go on and on as he does? I do declare he gets it from my aunt, Lady Catherine."

"One can hardly find fault in always being amiable."

"I imagine so, but would you not prefer amiability of a different sort. I, for one, can think of much more pleasurable ways to engage our mouths."

"What are you thinking, Mr. Darcy?"

"Let me show you."

Sitting up, Darcy pulled her into his lap. He began kissing her, initially upon her lips; he soon trailed his soft, warm lips to her earlobes, her neck, slowly and tenderly, lower and lower until he reached a most delectable spot to lavish his attentions. She wanted more than he eagerly bestowed. Elizabeth reached for his hand and guided it to her bosom hoping to encourage him to exercise less restraint. Pleased. Willing. Darcy's long fingers explored her curves.

Elizabeth moved to sit astride his lap, a shift that resulted in the pooling of her nightgown around her, fully exposing every inch of her bare thighs. With much less hesitation than before, Darcy caressed her, moving slowly up and down, inside and around. She leaned forward to impart soft kisses along his neckline, to every visible part of his chest. Elizabeth suspended her actions to remove his shirt, an undertaking in which he willingly assisted. She picked up where she had left off by kissing the spots that promised to melt his resistance as she brushed her body against his.

What did it matter to Elizabeth that she was as inexperienced in the art of seduction—as she also was in matters of the heart? She trusted him—trusted him instinctively to know that, once started, he would take her exactly where she needed to be. The remembrance of his body against hers, the touch of his hands and his soft lips upon her face, her lips, her breasts, every inch of her body, had been faithful in her private moments since their night at Pemberley. Just thinking of him evoked theretofore unexplained sensations throughout her body. Now he was right there. His closeness was overwhelmingly intoxicating. She yearned for every part of him.

He understood what she needed—what her heart and her body desired most; the exact same heartfelt desires and body aching needs had been his own constant companions for all the months since he first had laid eyes on her.

Though wanting to enjoy completion inside her more than anything, Darcy determined it best to bring things under control. He would not take the next step with Elizabeth that night, and certainly not at the parsonage. That would have to wait. The consummation of their love, without a doubt in his mind, would last throughout the night.

Still, the generous lover that he was, he saw no need to deny her pleasure. He would have to find his own relief later. He gently guided her to the floor and pushed her nightgown even higher.

* * *

Mr. and Mrs. Collins returned from Rosings late in one of Lady Catherine's carriages. The sound of the approaching carriage roused Darcy and Elizabeth from their slumber.

"I am sorry, my love. I had not intended to stay this long. I must go."

"But to leave now is to risk being detected. You may be able to silence the servants, but I dare say all the money in the world will not silence my cousin."

"You have a point there, my love. I will wait a bit longer, I suppose." As he reached for his shirt, he continued, "I am not inclined to remain in Kent after tonight though. Will you agree to shorten your visit and accompany me back to town in the morning?"

"Is it necessary to leave here so soon?"

"I believe it is, or at least it will be once I advise my aunt that we intend to marry. You will not be able to remain at the parsonage once she hears of our engagement."

"I suppose it would put my friend Charlotte in a most awkward position. Must we tell your aunt right away? Why not delay it for a few days?"

"No—it is better she hears it as soon as can be ... directly from me. I will speak with her first thing in the morning. Thereafter, I shall return here to bring you to town."

Elizabeth clapped her hands in jest. "You have done well, Mr. Darcy. You have decided all this on your own, with little to no involvement from me. Where have you decided I shall stay upon my return to town?"

"Where would you like to stay, Elizabeth? I will convey you to your relatives in Cheapside, if that is your wish. You have the option of staying at the Bingley townhouse or even at my townhouse, if that is something you are comfortable with."

"I will think on it. My preference is to remain with you. However, it might not be the best idea for us to reside in the same home out of wedlock."

"It is not unheard of, especially if we are discreet and marry quickly."

"I would prefer to have Jane present when we marry. Perhaps we should wait until we are in Hertfordshire for the wedding."

"We shall see."

"I am quite determined, Mr. Darcy."

"As am I."

They waited a short time longer until all footsteps parading outside in the hallway faded and it sounded as though the household was settled. With one last kiss and a long silent glance, Darcy picked up his jacket and headed for the door of Elizabeth's room. He turned to grant her one last soulful parting look.

Darcy was descending the stairway when he encountered another late-night wanderer ascending the stairs towards him, with a single candle in hand.

"Mrs. Collins, please excuse me."

Startled, but far from surprised, Charlotte said, "No—excuse me, Mr. Darcy." The quiet creak of the door confirmed he had left the house. Charlotte paused just outside of Elizabeth's bedchamber.

Well, well ... it is just as I supposed.

Chapter 24 – Shades of Pemberley

Lady Catherine was inconsolable, livid, and quite out of her mind. Like errant children, Darcy, Anne, and Richard sat in the drawing room and listened as she ranted on and on of disappointed hopes and dreams, misplaced loyalties and betrayals. Darcy understood why he was suffering her verbal abuse. So did Anne, to some degree. Richard had no idea why he had been forced to endure his aunt's tirade, except that she had demanded he remain in his seat. She knew not what he was guilty of, but her suspicion alone that he had a hand in the scheme was enough for her ladyship.

"You, Darcy, have used my Anne most ill, not to mention the degradation of your announcement to our family."

Anne could not deny that she had been encouraged by Darcy's attentions to her of late. She had warmed to the idea of a future with him, but only if it meant she would remain at Rosings. Rosings Park was her birthright after all. However, upon meeting the woman whom he loved, all such nonsensical notions she cast aside. She cared for her cousin too dearly to allow him to settle for her when his heart belonged to another.

"The inequality of fortune, the disparity of age, a widow—the Mistress of Pemberley! How dare you? Are you out of your mind?" Lady Catherine continued, "Connections in trade! Heaven and earth! Are the shades of Pemberley to be thus polluted?

"Do not think for one moment that I failed to take notice of how that impertinent Mrs. Elizabeth Calbry looked at you. How she reacted upon seeing you here in this very room. Wealthy young gentlemen do not marry women like that. They make them their mistresses! With a woman like that, one might have his cake and eat it too!

"You might have it all—Pemberley and Rosings! Marry Anne. Honour your duty to your family. Take Mrs. Calbry as your mistress, if you must, and set her up in her own establishment in town!"

Anne gasped! "Is that kind of marriage what you would wish for me?"

"Why on earth not? It is how it is done in our sphere. It was good enough for me; why should it not be good enough for my own daughter?"

"Because I want something more for myself, and at last I am free to pursue it—whatever it may be! I am relieved to no longer labour under the misapprehension that Fitzwilliam and I are engaged!"

"This is not to be borne. You three are the next generation of our distinguished family. If you persist in these foolish notions of going against tradition, honour, and duty, it will be the end of our family's extraordinary legacy. Darcy has attached himself to a widow whose family is entrenched in trade, despite her hint of respectability as a gentleman's daughter.

"What is your intention, Anne, to marry some gentleman farmer, a local physician or, heaven forbid, a country lawyer? Moreover, what of you, Fitzwilliam? How will this brazenness and lack of respect for family and tradition affect your choice of a bride? Shall I expect to hear that you, too, have set your sights on a penniless gentleman's daughter?"

That Lady Catherine was upset was evident for Anne, Richard, and Darcy to see. However, was that any excuse for her continued abuse of them over their own choices for their futures? Three young adults with their own lives to lead, choices to make and mistakes to endure, sat before her.

It had gone on long enough. Unwilling to suffer his aunt's abuse a moment longer, Darcy announced the matter settled. He was resolved upon marrying the woman he loved. Furthermore, he told his aunt that she was never to abuse his future wife again if she expected a continued association with him. With that, Richard and he bid their farewells and made way to the parsonage to meet Elizabeth.

Charlotte experienced emotions of every kind with Elizabeth's impending departure. Pleasure at having re-established their friendship, sorrow at having to part again so soon, elation that Elizabeth was engaged to such a worthy gentleman, and uncertainty of how the news of this would affect her ladyship's continued condescension towards Mr. Collins. However, the greatest of her emotions was that of joy and the two lifelong friends said good-bye with the agreement that Charlotte should plan to visit Pemberley in the coming months.

Darcy, Elizabeth, and Richard soon settled into the carriage and made their way towards town. By the time the carriage reached Bromley, Richard had suffered enough of the two lovers. Sensing the carriage had become a little too crowded for three, he elected to continue the remainder of the journey on horseback.

Once he noticed the drawn carriage shades, he felt no need for him to arrive in town at the same time as his cousin. He doubted whether he would be spending the night at the Darcy townhouse any time soon. He decided to ride on ahead, straight to his parents' townhouse, with the intention of heading them off before they resumed their journey from Matlock to Kent after a brief stay in town.

Not that either Darcy or Elizabeth was aware of what took place outside the carriage. After being sequestered with Richard for so long, they appreciated the time alone. They had been aware he was talking—but what he discussed, neither Darcy nor Elizabeth could say with any degree of certainty.

Darcy moved to Elizabeth's side of the carriage. He started removing the pins from her hair.

"You must allow me to apologise, for my staff will be ill prepared for our arrival."

"Excellent, then we shall skip the formalities, and I may join you in your apartment straightaway."

"Are you certain, my love? I am willing to wait until our wedding night."

"Do not dare tease me this way! Four weeks, I shall not bear it."

"So—you are quite adamant that we are not to marry as soon as possible?"

"Oh! Of that, I am sure. I have never met your aunt and uncle, and you have yet to meet all my relatives in town. We both must have a chance to reconsider if either does not suit," she teased.

"No—Never. I have your word. It is too late for misgivings. Besides, you have met Lady Catherine. I can safely say it does not get any worse than that."

"And I should imagine you will like my Uncle Gardiner as well, just as you professed to have enjoyed meeting my Aunt Gardiner, and their children are delightful. Therefore, it is settled. Neither of us will have cause for regrets, and we shall be the happiest couple in all of England." She ventured light kisses along the cleft of his chin. Encouraged, Darcy picked up where they had left off the night before.

He asked, "May I?" as he began to unbutton her spencer, revealing her cleavage. Elizabeth did not object.

Blessing her with soft kisses along her neckline and her face, Darcy raised the hem of her gown and traced his hand between her legs, close to her cherished spot repeatedly without giving in to her silent pleas for satisfaction. She quietly besought and attempted to drag his hand there. He did not give in to her demands. He continued his wonderfully tormenting diversion—caressing her hips, her belly, and her inner thighs. Repeatedly, the near brush of his hands increasingly aroused her. The more he teased and delayed, the greater became the hunger only his touch could feed.

When, at last, he heeded her body's whisper, her response was exquisite. The pleasure she felt—phenomenal. Covering her mouth with his, engulfing her in a deep, passionate kiss to stifle her every moans, all the while holding her, stilling her trembles, he paced his actions to prolong her pleasure as long as possible

With Elizabeth spent in his arms, Darcy whispered, "I am determined to remain by your side every moment until the wedding and forever thereafter. I never wish for us to be parted again."

Releasing a soft breath of completion, she concurred and soon drifted off into a quiet contented slumber and remained so for the rest of the journey.

Chapter 25 – Everything in my power

Elizabeth cried out at the momentary discomfort. Darcy paused. Astounded! "Elizabeth—have you ... you have never?" He was astonished as he looked upon her face and wiped the hint of tears from her eyes. He brushed her hair aside and whispered, "I am so sorry, my love. Shall we stop?"

"No—please, do not stop." She began to wiggle her body under his weight.

"Stop. Do not move just yet. Let us lie here awhile—until our bodies are accustomed. I do not wish to have you experience pain." He kissed her lips. "This will be wonderful, my love."

Later, Darcy cleansed Elizabeth's body himself and noticed the faint evidence of blood, the affirmation of her lost "maidenhood." Having completed his purposefully erotic yet delicate task, he joined her in his bed and drew her body close to him in a loving embrace.

"I wish I had known before. I suspected you lacked much experience, but ... why did you not tell me that the marriage was never consummated?"

"What would you have me say? I ... my ... the marriage WAS consummated, even if I had to suffer it only the one time."

"Only one time," he repeated slowly. "Do you recall what took place?"

"Sometimes, I fear I will never forget it."

"I will do everything in my power to make certain you do, but it might help to talk about it. Will you tell me what happened?"

Elizabeth reluctantly tore herself away from Darcy's embrace and sat up in bed. "He ... Daniel came to my room. He had been drinking heavily; my greatest recollection is the stench of brandy on his breath. He did not bother to disrobe. He lowered himself atop me and pushed my gown up." Elizabeth paused a moment. "After groping around with his trousers, he managed to push himself between my legs, repeatedly. After a few grunts, it was over. He rolled from me and made his way to his own room."

"Then what?"

"Then, I got up, cleansed myself, and returned to bed."

"And did you notice any blood?"

"No, why do you ask such a question?"

"Because, my love, when a woman gives herself to a man ... for the first time, some traces of blood might be expected."

"Always?"

"Perhaps not always ... but, my love, that is the way it was tonight ... between us," he whispered before pulling her onto the bed and kissing her passionately. After a spell, he made love to her once more, this time with more tenderness, more restraint, filling her completely until they lay spent in each other's embrace.

Darcy woke in the middle of the night with Elizabeth nestled in his arms, and a lingering thought. *She said she did not love her first husband, but never to have been loved by him... Whatever might have been the true nature of that marriage, I am her first, the first ... the only man to have won her heart and the only man to make love to her utterly and unconditionally.* Which such thoughts, it was difficult not to experience some satisfaction and hope that, God willing, he would be the only man to know her in that sense.

Surrounded by a flood of soft morning light, Elizabeth studied the beautiful man resting by her side. This was the first time she had ever awakened to find herself in bed with a gentleman. She prayed every morning would be that way, persuaded as she was that they should never be parted again.

Elizabeth stretched her arms above her head in warm contentment as she light-heartedly looked about Darcy's room. It was just what it ought to be ... refined and dignified, a perfect reflection of the owner's taste.

Nothing could have been better than to witness his smile when he awakened. She slid into his welcoming embrace.

"How are you this morning, my love?"

Elizabeth traced her fingers along his light stubble of a beard. After a quick brush of her lips against his, she snuggled into his arms.

"Will it always be this way? I mean to say, it was beautiful once we moved beyond the initial ... pain."

"My love, any pain or discomfort you felt will soon be a thing of the past. I promise. I am sorry again. I did not expect ... well, you know."

"Did I please you?"

"Beyond my wildest dreams, my love. Our first time together was everything I wished for and more, much more. Promise you will spend every night, henceforth, sharing my bed."

Darcy felt blessed to have spent the night with his beloved Elizabeth and to awaken with her next to him. He had waited so long for that moment. He did not wish to tear his eyes away from her face. She was the most magnificent creature he had ever beheld. Persuading her to lie on her back, he gently pushed her knees up to her chest. He knelt on the bed before her, bent forward, and encouraged her to wrap both legs around his waist. Elizabeth was captivated by his expressive eyes and unable to do anything other than as he silently commanded.

As he traced her lips, her neckline, the curves of her bosom with one hand, with the other, he stroked her inner thighs and teased her mercilessly with the hint of offering more. Having excited her amply, he began massaging her folds, and, gently stroking her arousal, pushed his fingers inside her, where he gratified her sacred spot. Swaying her hips hungrily, pushing against his hand, she urged him to press deeper.

Darcy had dreamed of loving her that way for months. Her explosive response was more than he could have imagined. Removing his hand, he entered her with a deep thrust, each captured by the look in the other's eyes. He moved her to keep pace with him. Her soft moans conspired with his own rich, melodious voice—promises that it would always be that way between them, affirmations of his undying love, and such vivid descriptions of her pleasures until waves of rapturous pleasure flooded her body.

Unable to restrain himself any longer, he soon succumbed in unadulterated surrender.

Hours later, urgent knocking interrupted Darcy and Elizabeth's slumber. He reluctantly tore himself away from her side to answer the door. His valet stood in the hallway with the message that Lord and Lady Matlock were downstairs and insisted upon seeing him at once.

"My aunt and uncle are here?" Darcy turned his attention to Elizabeth. His eyes bore a silent apology. He addressed the unfortunate messenger. "At this hour?"

"Yes, Sir. Mr. Grey informed them that you are not receiving callers today. They refuse to leave. What shall I do?"

"Have them wait for me in the drawing room." Darcy paused with the door half-closed. The house was short-staffed. "Will you see that they are attended while they wait, please? Thank you, Yves."

"Thank you, Sir. Again, I beg your pardon for the interruption."

Darcy returned to bed and sat beside Elizabeth, who had since donned her robe and sat up, her elbows resting against a pillow.

"I am sorry, my love. My uncle and aunt, Lord and Lady Matlock, are downstairs. They refuse to leave until they have spoken with me."

"Then I shall come with you."

"Are you positive that you wish to meet them under these circumstances? I mean—" He was not sure what to say. He had not counted upon his relatives meeting Elizabeth that way.

"I will have to meet them at some point. Why not get this over with; the sooner the better, do you not agree?"

"You are right, of course." He took her hands in his and bestowed a light kiss upon each of them. "I shall ring someone to assist you."

Within a half hour, Darcy and Elizabeth descended the staircase hand in hand. They braced themselves as they entered the drawing room.

Lady Matlock gasped! She was stunned. She never expected to see her nephew entertaining female company in his home at that hour. Darcy had allowed this woman to spend the night in his home, possibly his bed. What if Georgiana had come with them and had borne witness to the spectacle?

Her husband was the first to speak. "So, what Richard said is true! You and this woman—"

Darcy raised his hand. "Before you utter another word, allow me to introduce you to Mrs. Elizabeth—" Darcy's introduction halted with a swishing of exquisite, silken fabrics and a thump.

Lady Matlock had collapsed!

Chapter 26 – The censure of the world

Just days before, despite the lateness of the afternoon, upon their arrival in London, Darcy headed straightaway to acquire a special licence. Meaning to have his way, Darcy spared no expense. Soon enough, his fondest wish had come true.

As it happened, all of Elizabeth's resolve had melted with Darcy's plea that he not be obliged to introduce her as the wife of the late Mr. Calbry for any length of time. He wanted the world to know she was his. Though she teased him of being selfish, she allowed herself to be persuaded. As he had promised her, she too had promised him that she would do anything in her power to make certain of his happiness. With no one else to satisfy other than each other on something of utmost importance to Darcy, it was a matter easily settled.

* * *

Darcy and his incensed uncle stood opposite each other in his study. "The odds are stacked against you. Everyone who knows you would have counselled against this. Is that why you rushed into this marriage?

"What could have possessed you to rush into matrimony with a dowerless widow when you, one of the most eligible gentlemen of Society, could have chosen a bride from the most wealthy, the most beautiful and refined young ladies of the *ton*."

"I do not believe we rushed into anything. I offered my hand to her months ago, though unsuccessfully. We have since had time to know what it is like being apart when in our hearts we long to be together."

"What woman would deny you? Is this truly love on your part or have you married her to prove to yourself that you can have her? If it is simply lust, then you might as easily have taken her as your mistress."

"Do you think so little of me? I would never have broached the subject. She is a gentlewoman whom I love and respect. I have admired her for as long as I have known her. I am honoured she accepted my hand in marriage. I will cherish and protect her, and I will not allow anyone to disparage her."

"Of course, I apologise for any offence. Moreover, I would expect no less of you. You are still a young man. So much of life is before you.

"Too often, when a man of your age makes such a choice, it proves to be unwise. I pray you will not come to regret this step you have taken," he said as he approached Darcy with an extended hand. "You will always have the love and support of your family."

Elizabeth had remained in the drawing room with Darcy's aunt while the gentlemen talked. Her ladyship apologised for her exaggerated response to Elizabeth's presence in Darcy's home. No, she suffered no affliction; she was upset. She believed Darcy was entertaining his mistress in his home—in Georgiana's home. Elizabeth accepted the apology in the spirit it was given. Lady Matlock knew, as well as anyone, that the Darcys would need the support of the Fitzwilliam family against the censure of the world and, most particularly, the London *ton*. A united front was called for from that moment on, and so it would be.

Prior to their departure, Darcy told his aunt and uncle that he had intended to call upon them soon, but he simply wanted time alone with his bride for now. He begged their indulgence. They parted with the agreement that the Darcys would dine with them at the Matlock townhouse in a matter of days.

After an entire week of blissful seclusion, the Darcys decided to venture out of doors. Elizabeth had written to Jane and Charlotte the day after the marriage, and not a moment too soon, for almost immediately thereupon, the news of the union was read in the *Post*.

They deemed only two social calls as important. First, Darcy and Elizabeth called upon the Gardiners in Cheapside. As foretold by Elizabeth, Darcy was much obliged to meet her uncle and to renew his ac-

quaintance with Mrs. Gardiner. The children, he indeed found delightful.

Second, Darcy and Elizabeth dined with Lord and Lady Matlock.
Georgiana was enthusiastic over her brother's choice. As much as she
liked her cousin Anne and valued their friendship, she could tell her
brother was as happy as he had ever been, having won the hand of the
woman that he loved. Though it had been decided that Georgiana
would remain with her aunt and uncle for a while longer, she would
soon return to Pemberley to live with her brother and her new sister.

Chapter 27 – No improper pride

The Darcys arrived at Netherfield Park to less than joyous circumstances. Just the day before, Mr. Bennet had taken a fall from his horse. Despite his age, he had suffered some measure of pride in his ability to walk away from the incident without a scratch. How fortuitous he felt in having been spared the burden of seeing a doctor. He climbed into bed, earlier than had been his wont, with the certainty that the next day would mean the end of his aches and pains, especially the pounding in his head.

Jane, having not been downstairs to receive the Darcys, knocked on Elizabeth's bedchamber door. Elizabeth opened the door and, shocked by the sight of her sister on the verge of tears, embraced her.

"Dearest Jane, is everything all right?"

"My dear Lizzy, I am so sorry to leave on the heels of your arrival. I must be off to Longbourn. I received word our father has lost consciousness." Elizabeth nearly gasped aloud before schooling her demeanour. Jane noticed. "It would mean the world to me if you would come with me. Please come—I beg of you."

"No, Jane. You know I cannot accompany you there."

"But Lizzy!"

"No, Jane!"

Darcy witnessed the exchange with considerable consternation. What was his wife about, that she should not wish to visit her own father during such a time? Jane was getting nowhere with his wife.

Darcy stood from his chair and walked towards the two sisters. He placed both hands upon his wife's shoulders and pressed gently.

"Mrs. Bingley, this is grave news. I am sorry. You and Charles should go on ahead. Do not fret. Elizabeth and I will soon follow." Elizabeth's shoulders tensed despite the firm hands resting upon them.

"Thank you, Mr. Darcy." Jane curtsied and turned to quit the room. "Thank you."

Darcy had suspected Elizabeth was not particularly close to either of her parents, though he never knew the extent of that distance. Alone with Elizabeth, Darcy pressed on until he learnt the whole story behind her first marriage. She confessed all—the scandal, her father's lack of support, her late husband's callous disregard and adulterous behaviour, and her in-laws' contempt.

Elizabeth's account was beyond anything he had imagined, by far. He believed she had married a sensible man whom she simply did not love, when, in fact, she had been married to a scoundrel, an adulterer, and a fool.

"Elizabeth, you have suffered greatly. Indeed, I had no idea, my love. Surely, you must see…you must know… that in failing to forgive your father, you are continuing to hold on to the pain of the past. You need to let go of this acrimony."

"No—I am afraid you do not understand what it is like to lose the esteem for a parent."

"I understand." Darcy took her hand in his. "I spent years being angry with my father, angry with him because he failed to bestow the same favour towards Georgiana and me that he heaped upon George Wickham. It was not until he had fallen ill—too ill to handle the day-to-day management of Pemberley—and had started to hand the reins to me that I began to release my anger and accept my father for the man he was. I cannot imagine how it would have been had I never forgiven him and held firm to resentment and pain until it was too late.

"Do not let such a fate befall you, my Elizabeth. Visit your father, show him that you have forgiven him and bear him no ill will for mistakes of the past.

"He may be the only grandfather our children will ever know."

"I will think on it. I feel I am not ready."

"You heard your sister, Elizabeth. If not now, when?"

Darcy's words to Elizabeth had proved convincing. He agreed to accompany her to Longbourn, to remain with her for the entirety of that important step in reconciling the past.

Upon their arrival, the entire household was in disarray. Mrs. Bennet was in despair. What if Mr. Bennet should die? What was to become of them? Darcy tried to reassure her that he would protect and provide for them.

Mrs. Bennet was distressed. Forced to leave Longbourn, their home? How should she ever recover? Darcy said he would convince Mr. Collins to sell; otherwise, he would purchase another home nearby.

Mrs. Bennet was distracted. Lizzy married ... a house in town ... Mistress of Pemberley ... married by special licence. Darcy prayed for a miracle.

Elizabeth pulled a chair up to his bedside when it was her turn to sit with her father. She placed her hand upon his and voiced her sentiments aloud.

"I am here, Papa." She paused a long while, gathering her thoughts.

"First, I forgive you. I must beg of your forgiveness, as well. I have been such a fool, stubborn and headstrong on this matter. If I have any defence at all, it is that I was angry that you would not allow me to tell you my side of the story, to tell you of Daniel's true character. In the end, it may have made no difference at all, but at least I would have believed you respected me.

"But, enough of the past, what is done is done. You recall my philosophy to think of the past as its remembrance brings me pleasure. I say it is time I adhere to those sentiments I have trumpeted for so long. Do you not agree?

"Oh Papa, I am so happy! I have remarried. He is the best man in the world. You know him already. I am married to Mr. Darcy of Pemberley and Derbyshire, Charles's closest friend. You may remember he visited Charles at Netherfield this past winter.

"Now, before you go thinking to yourself that I am out of my senses accepting such a proud and unpleasant sort of man, let me assure you of my attachment to him. I love him. Indeed, he has no improper pride. He is perfectly amiable.

"Papa, if you could only know what he is truly like, what he has done." Elizabeth then told her father all Darcy had done for Lydia. She continued, "So wake up, Papa. I wish for you to get to know my husband, enjoy a part of our lives. Come visit us at Pemberley. I have seen Mr. Darcy's magnificent library for myself. You will love it."

Elizabeth became aware of a gentle pressure upon her hand. The tears that had been on the verge of shedding, fell from her eyes as she realised it was her father's own hand now resting upon hers.

Days later, with Mr. Bennet having turned the corner and steadily improving, Jane and Elizabeth found time to catch up with each other and to begin planning the long-delayed wedding celebration. Jane broached the question foremost on her mind.

"Lizzy, why on earth did you two rush into the marriage? Why not have waited a few days, even a week so the wedding might take place with the family?"

"Oh! Jane, I wanted you beside me, and Charles as well, but Fitzwilliam vowed he would not consummate our relationship out of wedlock. What was I to do? What would you have done in my situation?"

"Shame on you, Lizzy! I think you had better come up with a more fitting excuse than that," Jane chided before the two broke out in a bout of infectious laughter.

* * *

With each day, the Netherfield and Longbourn households settled into a comfortable routine, with the occupants of each passing back and forth regularly. Still, Darcy and Elizabeth found ample time for themselves.

Darcy and Elizabeth walked about the lane, arm in arm, one pleasant afternoon.

"You must know these parts like the back of your hand, dearest. I long for an out-of-the-way spot in which a young man violently in love with his lady might escape to show her the extent of his affections and esteem."

"Indeed, I believe I know just the place, Mr. Darcy."

"Then by all means, lead on, my love."

They soon came upon said place. It was as private as he had hoped, and he successfully endeavoured to keep her in the secluded oasis for several hours.

Upon their return to the house, they walked along, hands entwined, with some discussion of their immediate plans. Darcy was happy to see Elizabeth getting along with her father and could easily judge for himself what an uplifting it beget in her spirits. When asked how much longer before they must depart for Derbyshire, he said, "We will remain in Hertfordshire until your father is up and about."

"You would make such a sacrifice—for me?"

"Yes, my darling Elizabeth. I would do that and far more for you."

"I cannot help but feel guilty in remaining in Hertfordshire for so long and keeping you from your beloved home."

"My love, might I remind you that it is now *our* home and I spend less than half of my time at Pemberley, especially over the past two years. We have time enough to return—for me to resume my responsibilities as Master and for you to assume your role as Mistress."

"Regardless of where we are, I would hope you will find yourself at home wherever I am, just as I feel with you already."

"Indeed. I feel it too."

Thus, the Darcys would remain at Netherfield a while longer as Mr. Bennet continued to reclaim his health.

* * *

The wedding celebration hosted by the Bingleys at Netherfield, in the Darcys' honour, was splendid. More grand and elegant than a dinner party, it was less extravagant than a formal ball. Friends and family alike attended. Mr. Bennet's presence was an added blessing. His demeanour was open, engaging, and far less cynical than was his wont. Darcy and he spoke at length, much to Elizabeth's delight.

The invitation to the Hurst household was unavoidable. During that time of year, it was wholly unfashionable to be in town. With no better place to be, their acceptance was wholehearted. Caroline was not as condescending towards Elizabeth as she might have been. She looked forward to returning to Pemberley, and she told the Darcys so, more than once. Mr. Hurst was as he ever was. Louisa was not herself —she behaved rather oddly.

Despite being guests of honour, the couple did not remain in the company of the party revellers for long.

That night in bed, settled into a comfortable embrace, Elizabeth whispered, "I love it when you love me like this."

Darcy massaged her back with his fingertips. "You love it," his deep voice resounded tenderly in her ear, "I love it. I could stay here inside you," he brushed his lips against hers, "and love you like this forever."

"Indeed." Elizabeth returned his warm gesture with a deep, probing kiss. "This position favours such an endeavour."

"Indeed," he whispered back, "my favourite position, my love."

"Have you any other favourite things I should know about?"

"Just one—you should know that you are my favourite person, Elizabeth."

The sound of her name, resonating from his lips while they made love, always proved too powerful for Elizabeth to resist. Talk ceased. They relived the unforgettable experience of their first night as man and wife.

Chapter 28 – Such an assembly as this

The dimly lighted crowded room combined with the sweltering air, causing him to tug at his crisp white cravat. The loud, poorly orchestrated music assaulted his senses. The less than impressive garments and adornments worn by men and women alike had to have been the gaudiest and most unfashionable he had ever seen.

Good heavens, I am a long way from Grosvenor Square. Standing in the shadows, he looked about the room. *Why in the world did I agree to attend such an assembly as this?*

He need not look far for the reason for his present discomfort. Once again, Elizabeth found herself at a lively party, in the audience of the married, the widowed, and the confirmed spinsters, but never before had she managed it with such a spirit of contentment. She did not blush during the brazen whisperings of the proclivities of men. Neither did she lend anything to the conversation. However, on some topics, she could hardly contain her smiles.

A devastatingly handsome young gentleman approached her. He purposely chose her from the crowd of women, with no concern for the eager ladies in his path who might have felt slighted.

"Miss Elizabeth Bennet of Longbourn, I presume." He reached for her hand and bestowed a lingering kiss. Surprised, Elizabeth knew not what to say.

The striking gentleman continued. "Pardon me, madam, but I have been admiring your elegance, your beauty, and most of all, your stunning eyes from across the room for far too long.

"I have thereby taken it upon myself to make your acquaintance and request your hand for the next set." He did not await her reply. He led her to the dance floor.

They spoke not a word. Throughout the dance, he moved just a little too close, held her hands a little too long.

Elizabeth danced with him in stunned silence. Finally, she spoke. "Sir, I must warn you. My husband is here. He will take exception to the liberties you are taking with his wife."

"If you mean the tall, astoundingly handsome, but rather pompous young man who spent a great deal of time standing about looking stupid earlier this evening, do not worry about him. He has gone. I am here to take his place."

"Take his place?" Elizabeth's dark eyes widen. "Surely, you jest. I have grown rather fond of him. What shall I do with you?"

"Come home with me," he dared to whisper in her ear, on the assembly floor for all of Meryton to see.

"Home?"

"Come to Pemberley."

* * *

Riding along in the carriage, on the journey to Derbyshire, Darcy tucked her arm into his own and smiled down upon her before favouring her with a light kiss upon the tip of her nose.

Elizabeth returned his smile with a brilliant smile of her own. *I feel blessed in sharing my life with this man. This man who knows how to love me and says all the things I need to hear. This man who has given me so much—everything I have missed in my life and more.*

Surely, I shall never get enough of his loveliness, his sensitivity, his passion.

Therefore, it was and so it would always be—continuing tales of matrimonial bliss. Though she had no remembrance of her first wedding ceremony, having relegated it to the recesses of her mind, Mrs. Elizabeth Darcy would forever recall her joyousness that magical autumn evening, when she and Darcy stood before the officiant.

Rarely had she heard anything more beautifully spoken, commencing with the words from the Book of Common Prayer, "Dearly beloved. We are gathered together here ...."

And ending that night, with Darcy's own words, "Henceforth, you are mine and mine alone. I love you, dearest, loveliest Elizabeth."

Acknowledgements

The highest praise goes to Miss Jane Austen's timeless works, as well as the JAFF community and its curiosity to ask, "What if?"

Other *Pride and Prejudice* Variations
by
P O Dixon

To Have His Cake (and Eat It Too)
Mr. Darcy's Tale

What He Would Not Do
Mr. Darcy's Tale Continues

He Taught Me to Hope
Darcy and the Young Knight's Quest

Author Bio

P O Dixon writes *Pride and Prejudice* adaptations with one overriding purpose in mind—falling in love with Darcy and Elizabeth. Sometimes provocative, always entertaining, her stories are read, commented on, and thoroughly enjoyed by thousands of readers worldwide.

Her initial exposure to *Pride and Prejudice* was in 2007. After watching the 2005 film at least two times a day for as many weeks, she determined she needed to know much more of the story's hero. After reading the novel, along with several excellent 'what-if' books that told the story from Mr. Darcy's perspective, she came across a link to the online JAFF community. Her life has never been quite the same.

Discover much more at PODixon.com

13354404R00128

Made in the USA
Lexington, KY
26 January 2012